THE BOOK OF THE DEAD

Robert Richardson was born in Manchester in 1940. Since 1960 he has been a journalist, working for many years on the *Daily Mail* and contributing to, among others, the *Independent*, the *Guardian* and the *Sunday Times*. He is married with two sons and lives in Old Hatfield. Robert Richardson is also the author of *The Latimer Mercy*, *Bellringer Street* and *The Dying of the Light*, all of which are published by Gollancz.

D0370054

Also by Robert Richardson in Gollancz Crime

THE LATIMER MERCY
BELLRINGER STREET

THE BOOK OF
THE DEAD

by

Robert Richardson

GOLLANCZ CRIME

Gollancz Crime is an imprint of Victor Gollancz Ltd
14 Henrietta Street, London WC2E 8QJ

First published in Great Britain 1989
by Victor Gollancz Ltd

First Gollancz Crime edition 1990

British Library Cataloguing in Publication Data
Richardson, Robert *1934—*
    The book of the dead.
    I. Title
    823.914 [F]

    ISBN 0-575-04888-3

Printed and bound in Great Britain
by Cox & Wyman Ltd, Reading

For Colin and 'Titia

Author's apology

Having writers as friends means they may borrow your neighbourhood, your village or even your home as the setting for a book; in this instance, all three have been used. It must be stressed, therefore, that here are no real people or actual events, but imaginary wickedness connected with a surprising appearance of Sherlock Holmes. The only reality lies in the backdrop of the Lake District locations, although Attwater does not exist under that name.

Chapter One

Leaden October light was dying over the coastal plain of Lancashire as a menacing Valkyrie sky marched in from the sea, iron-black fists of cloud spuming out of a cauldron of lurid sulphur. Driving north along the M6, Augustus Maltravers apprehensively watched its approach for half an hour until, just beyond Lancaster, the storm rushed in and detonated above him. His car gave its initial hiccup as a scatter of rain hurled glistening sequins across the windscreen and almost instantaneously he was engulfed in a pelting downpour, the silver beams of his headlights picking up the crashing torrent as it hammered the motorway ahead and bounced back violently. He optimistically ignored whatever had caused the momentary splutter and pressed on, windscreen wipers clicking from right to left in frantic arcs. Above the kettledrum tattoo on the car roof, he heard a booming groan of thunder stride across the sky as his engine stumbled again. By the time he entered what he still thought of as Westmorland, despite the county having regained its ancient name of Cumbria, he was peering through saturated darkness and conditions beneath the bonnet were becoming critical.

Protesting constantly, the car staggered off at the Kendal exit and finally expired on an empty stretch of unlit country road midway between two villages. Maltravers swore comprehensively and looked gloomily out of the window. To his right, the rise of a hill vanished into a curtain of rain and to his left a field of dark wet emptiness stretched beyond a Lakeland stone wall. The earlier violence of the torrent had eased, but the relentless downpour that persisted would do wonders for shares in the ark-building industry. As far as he could calculate, he was about four miles from

Brook Cottage. Any garages still open would have sent their mechanics home and calling out the AA — a rescue organisation without whose protection he would not venture a mile on any road — would mean an indefinite and probably lengthy wait.

The only option appeared to be walking to the village some distance ahead where there should be a telephone from which he could ring Malcolm and ask him to come to his rescue. As Maltravers stepped out, the rain made a quite unnecessary extra effort and it was like standing under a high pressure shower as he fumbled to haul things from the boot. By the time he had found his raincoat, the back of his blazer was soaked through to his shirt and short brown hair was plastered to his head like seaweed on a wave-washed boulder. He dragged out his suitcase and umbrella, slammed the boot shut, then paused to wipe the worst of the rain from a lean face that would have been handsome except for a fractional lopsidedness about the axis of a Grecian nose. Polished cornflower blue eyes squinted with philosophical resignation as he trudged off towards the village, a tall, slightly ridiculous figure in the night.

After a few minutes he heard a car approaching from behind and raised his umbrella plaintively, but the vehicle swept past, hissing through a puddle which swelled out into a shell-shaped cascade, soaking him from knees to ankles. Maltravers looked dejectedly at his sopping trousers and sighed, accepting that it must be St Christopher's night off. He noticed an old milepost half hidden in the long grass by the roadside and crouched down to read the legend carved into the stone: Attwater 3 miles. At least there was the village before that, although there was no sign he was yet anywhere near it. He straightened up and plodded soddenly on, indifferent to the possibility of meeting a river he would have to ford; it was inconceivable that he could be made any wetter.

Two other passing cars ignored him before a high wall loomed out of the murkiness as the road curved to his left. He followed it to a pair of iron gates with a brass plate bearing the name Carwelton Hall screwed to the brickwork. There was no indication that what appeared to be an old manor house had now become the headquarters of the electricity board or some similar undertaking and lights were shining in the downstairs rooms thirty feet beyond the gates. Clearly such premises must contain a telephone and he could surely persuade the occupants that he was genuinely in need of help and not a passing homicidal maniac. One of the gates squeaked as he opened and closed it behind him, then he squelched along the drive and up ten wide, curved steps. The front door looked at least a hundred years old, but there was a modern bell push which sounded a strident ring when he tried it.

As he waited, wild nocturnal elements and mock Gothic architecture conjured up in his mind several possible welcomes he might receive. An old, twisted and clearly mad woman still serving meals to the corpse of her husband, rigid in wing collar and frock coat, in his chair at the candlelit dining-table; a forbidding butler, accompanied by a savage dog, peering uncertainly at him before hysterically crying that the Young Master had returned; a sinister figure in full evening dress unnervingly assuring him that he was expected and really must see the cask of amontillado in the cellar. Maltravers's embryonic writer's imagination had been fed and fattened in his youth by an endless diet of classic horror stories.

Then the door opened and he found himself faced by a slender redhead wearing designer jeans and a cream silk shirt with a chunky necklace of wooden beads the size of acorns. She looked at him for a moment then smiled sympathetically.

"Oh dear, you *are* wet aren't you?"

"Very," he replied. "And trying to say that drily is as near as I can manage to the condition. I'm sorry to trouble you, but my car's broken down and I want to call the people I'm visiting so they can collect me. Can I possibly use your telephone?"

"Who is it, Jennifer?" The man's voice came from beyond an open door off the brightly lit hall.

"Someone who needs the phone," she called back. "His car's packed up." She smiled at Maltravers again. "You'd better come in."

Leaving his dripping umbrella and case in the porch, Maltravers stepped inside and was wiping his soaking shoes on the mat as the man appeared. He appeared to be about sixty, his hair swept back from his forehead in waves of coal and slate above a strong, direct face, dark flesh like bunched muscles with a blue-grey shadow of evening stubble. The open-necked shirt, casual slacks and espadrilles would have looked bizarre on most men his age, but he retained a vigour preserved from his youth which carried it off.

"This is no night to be out in is it?" Fox brown eyes flickered with commiseration.

"It's not one I'd have chosen given the chance," Maltravers agreed. "It's very kind of you to help. My friends only live in Attwater so they can be here in a few minutes."

"Attwater?" The man sounded interested. "We know several people there. Where exactly?"

"Brook Cottage. Malcolm and Lucinda Stapleton."

"Malcolm and Lucinda?" There was unexpected recognition in the repetition. "You're not Augustus Maltravers, are you?"

Maltravers stared in surprise. "Yes, but how do you know that? Or does everyone know who's having visitors in the country?"

"No, but you're having dinner here tomorrow evening." He smiled at Maltravers's further look of confusion. "Malcolm told me you were visiting them and I insisted that you all come. I think I've read everything you've written and I've wanted to meet you for a long time."

"Thank you," Maltravers said. "Long arm of coincidence I suppose."

"Something like that." The man held out his hand. "I'm Charles Carrington and this is my wife Jennifer."

As they shook hands, Maltravers automatically glanced at the girl again. Seen properly in the full light of the hall, she was strikingly attractive, the elfin face with thin, deep pink lips framed by polished copper hair parted in the centre and flicked outwards at her shoulders. She was certainly no older than he had first supposed, which was considerably younger than her husband.

"My second wife," Carrington added, catching the expression that flashed across Maltravers's face. "Most people look surprised."

Maltravers felt uncomfortable. "I'm sorry, but I did rather suppose . . ."

"That she was my daughter perhaps?" Carrington interrupted. "Don't apologise, I'm quite used to it. However, there's no need to call Malcolm out on a night like this. I can run you up to Brook Cottage."

"That's putting you to too much trouble . . ." Maltravers protested.

"Not at all," Carrington insisted. "Wait here and I'll bring the Land Rover round. We'd offer you a drink, but I imagine you'd rather get straight to the cottage and change."

He disappeared through a door leading to the back of the house, leaving Maltravers with the second Mrs Carrington. He glanced round the panelled hall, dominated by a massive staircase with huge family portraits rising above mahogany banisters. Pale lemon Regency wallpaper and white painted ceilings alleviated heavy, dark brown woodwork. The electric lights were modern, but their shining brass fittings had been tastefully chosen to blend with their setting.

"Lovely house you have," he commented. "Have you lived here long?"

"Oh, Charles's family has been here for ever," she replied. "But it's only been my home since we married eighteen months ago. You should have seen it when I arrived. I've had a lot of fun cheering it up."

"It looks as if it could have been the sort of place which would have had a Mrs Danvers waiting to greet you," Maltravers observed wrily.

Jennifer Carrington laughed. "No, but it was like a tomb. All I wanted to do was put some life back into it."

"Really? Why had the life gone out?"

"There had been too much death in it." She looked apologetic. "Oh, God, doesn't that sound melodramatic? Anyway, you don't want to hear family history. Are you up here on holiday?"

"Partly, although I've also been commissioned to do an interview for the *Independent* with a retired actress who lives at Bowness, which means I'm getting paid for coming," he replied. "Then I've got to finish a new play to meet my agent's deadline. After that, it's a holiday."

"Charles really has been looking forward to meeting you. He was delighted when Malcolm told him you were a friend of theirs."

"I'm always flattered to discover fans. They're in short supply and . . ." Maltravers was interrupted by the sound of a vehicle on the gravel outside. Jennifer Carrington opened the door again to reveal a Land Rover, canvas hood glistening with rain in the light from the hall, waiting at the foot of the steps.

"I'll ring Brook Cottage and say you're on your way," she promised. "I'm sure you'll be drier when you come tomorrow."

"That won't be difficult." Maltravers looked at the small pool of rainwater gathered around his feet on the parquet floor. "Sorry about that. Thank you, and I look forward to meeting you again."

He pushed his case and umbrella into the back of the vehicle then climbed in and sat next to Carrington.

"Where did you abandon your car?" he asked as he drove into the road through another gate leading to a modern double garage next to the Hall.

"About a mile or so back towards the motorway," said Maltravers. "I'll call a mechanic out in the morning. It's probably nothing serious, but all I know about cars is that you put petrol in one end and an ignition key in the other."

After a few minutes Carrington wiped condensation off the inside of the windscreen with the back of his glove, peering through the rain and darkness for the village signpost at the turn just before Brook Cottage. He saw it and drove past then spun the wheel and the Land Rover rocked through the farmyard leading to the tiny unmarked lane no stranger would have discovered. Branches of dripping hedges rising over stone walls brushed the sides of the vehicle as they drove up the hill towards the cluster of homes in a hollow of the land. Carrington stopped by a small circular green with a patch of pampas grass surrounded by a ring of low box hedge at its centre. Opposite was the white pebbledash wall of Brook Cottage with its narrow strip of front garden which formed the boundary of the lane, a light glowing in the gable-end porch over the door.

"Incidentally, I've got something to show you tomorrow night," he said as Maltravers thanked him and started to get out. "Malcolm told me you're a great fan of detective fiction. I'm sure you'll be interested in a Sherlock Holmes story by Conan Doyle you've never read."

Maltravers paused and glanced at him in surprise as he reached into the back for his case and umbrella.

"More than interested, I'd be amazed. I've read all of them."

"Not this one," Carrington said with conviction. "There's an odd story behind it. Anyway there's Malcolm. See you tomorrow."

Maltravers stepped out then stood watching the Land Rover disappear back down the lane, rear lights like fire in rubies as Carrington braked for the bend. A new Sherlock Holmes. . . ?

"Now you've got this far, you can surely manage the last five yards," Malcolm called from the lighted doorway. "I told you last time you were here it was time you changed that car of yours."

Maltravers picked his way between puddles, an academic exercise in his condition. Lucinda appeared behind her husband, holding a glass which she held out towards him.

"Hot toddy, and we started running the bath when Jennifer rang."

Maltravers took the drink and cautiously leaned his dripping figure forward to kiss her.

"God bless you, lady," he said. "You have just saved the life of a minor literary talent, which is just as well because I haven't finished my complete works yet."

Three quarters of an hour later, bathed and changed, Maltravers went downstairs and into the low, square living-room. Outside, the wind had regathered and rain was impotently battering three foot thick granite walls that would have been indifferent to a hurricane. Pairs of red-shaded lights gleamed warmly in brass brackets fixed to rough white plaster and logs crackled and spat in the iron fire box of the open grate, the gale occasionally blowing back plumes of brown smoke as it curled up through the hammered steel chimney hood. The furniture included a baby grand piano, open top catching the light, a plump chesterfield sofa and matching easy chairs with cream linen loose covers patterned with leaves and a polished oak captain's seat which Maltravers secretly coveted. Rugs lay like islands of dark moss and rust in the grey sea of the flagged floor. Malcolm took his empty glass and went to the deep, well-stocked drinks cupboard built into one wall.

"The first one was medicinal," he said as he handed the tumbler back. "This one is social. Good to see you again."

Maltravers's only complaint about his hosts was that they lived too far from London for him to accept their standing invitation to visit whenever he wished more frequently. He had met Malcolm Stapleton during his journalistic career as a reporter in the Manchester offices of the *Daily Mail*. Malcolm had been offered a job several times on Fleet Street — as it then was — but had chosen to stay in his native north of England, becoming editor of the weekly *Cumbrian Chronicle* in Kendal. Stockily built with a mane of hair still packed thick as the bristles of a new brush, his square, cheerful face was permanently weathered by walks on the fells. He was also the most gifted amateur pianist Maltravers knew. He and Lucinda had two grown-up sons, the emerging craftsman Adrian at college studying furniture design and Simon training to be a building society manager.

"It's nice to be here." Maltravers raised the glass briefly as he went and stood by the fire. "Although I've had better journeys."

"Odd that you should have stopped at Carwelton Hall," said Malcolm. "Did Charles mention we're going there tomorrow night?"

"Yes. But I've never heard you talk about them and I thought I'd met most of your friends up here."

"We only got to know Charles and Jennifer about a year ago." Lucinda appeared at the top of the three shallow steps from the living-room into the kitchen, where she had been finishing off Lancashire hot pot and jacket potatoes. "You'll have noticed that they're not the average married couple."

Maltravers grinned at the overtones in her voice. The daughter of a successful Manchester businessman, Lucinda Stapleton combined all the sophistication of a city-bred childhood with the acquired common-sense abilities of an adopted countrywoman. Part-time teaching, involvement in countless village activities and the social side of being an editor's wife would have left lesser women exhausted; with her ash blonde hair folded back like a bird's wings about her crisp, intelligent face, in her corduroy skirt and flowered shirt, she looked quite capable of either setting off for a ten-mile hike or arranging an instant dinner party for a dozen unexpected guests.

"Not only did I notice, I'm afraid it showed," he replied. "She must be — what? — at least thirty years younger than him."

"Plus VAT," said Lucinda. "Come on, dinner's ready. We'll tell you about them while we eat."

Maltravers suspected that the hot pot contained at least half a cow and the product of a small vegetable patch; the muscular appetites of the north always defeated him and he refused a second helping after he had worked his way through the first with difficulty as he learned more about Charles Carrington. His first wife had died some years earlier, the first of a shattering series of personal tragedies. His son had been killed while climbing in the Cairngorms less than a year after his mother's death, then his daughter had moved to Manchester, where she had become fatally caught in the city's drug culture. She had been jailed twice, helplessly sliding from cannabis to cocaine to mainlining heroin. She had died from an overdose and her poisoned body had rotted in a squat in a filthy flat in the Moss Side district for a week before it was discovered.

Carrington had brought his daughter home after she was first released from prison, but when she ran away again and went back on drugs he had refused to have anything more to do with her. The last time he had seen her was when he had identified her corpse, but he had not regarded the body in the police mortuary as Gillian; it had been a stranger, totally unconnected with the child he had loved. He had used his legal influence to persuade the coroner to accept his evidence in writing so that he would not have to attend an inquest into the death of someone he had ceased to know. He had never even tried to discover what the verdict had been.

Embittered by her behaviour following the two deaths that had already almost broken him, he had obsessively absorbed himself in his legal work, becoming almost a recluse at Carwelton Hall which his family had owned for more than three centuries. Then a girl called Jennifer Lloyd had arrived in his life.

"It was before we got to know him, of course," Lucinda said, offering an alternative between meringues and Bakewell tart for a dessert which Maltravers could not even contemplate. "He's told us that she was very sympathetic and understanding and they were married within six months."

"All very romantic," commented Maltravers. "But can crabbed age and youth live together?"

"He's not that old," Lucinda corrected. "In fact he's very well preserved for sixty-odd. But . . . well there is gossip."

"There would be," Maltravers said sourly. "Whether or not there was any substance to it."

"Ah, but there is substance," Lucinda glanced across the table at her husband. "Isn't there?"

"I'm afraid so," Malcolm confirmed. "Jennifer is having an affair."

"Really?" Maltravers raised his eyebrows caustically. "How very boring and predictable. Do you know who with?"

"Someone called Duggie Lydden," Lucinda said. "He runs a not very successful interior design business in Kendal. That is when he can spare time from his girlfriends. He'll go for anything wearing a skirt."

"Then he should avoid Scotland," Maltravers remarked. "How long is this supposed to have been going on?"

"I became certain about three months ago, but it's probably more than that. According to somebody I know, it started not all that long after the marriage." Lucinda stood up. "Come on, we'll have coffee in the other room."

As they went through, Maltravers reflected that on very brief acquaintance, Charles Carrington had struck him as a decent man; after what he now knew he had suffered, he deserved better than a young wife who jumped into bed with a lover at the first opportunity.

"Does Carrington know what's going on?" He dipped into the dish of Kendal mint cake on the table beside him as Lucinda handed him his cup.

"I'm not sure." She sat down next to Malcolm on the chester-field, kicking off her shoes and tucking long legs beneath her.

"Husbands can be terribly blind about these things. One of Duggie's other affairs has been going on for ages."

Maltravers sipped his coffee. "You know, you're quite destroying my faith in the innocence of country living. There's quite enough of this sort of thing in London without it breaking out here as well."

"Don't be ridiculous," Malcolm told him. "I bet you can quote what Sherlock Holmes had to say about that."

"'It is my belief, Watson, founded upon my experience, that the lowest and vilest alleys of London do not present a more dreadful record of sin than does the smiling and beautiful countryside'," Maltravers said on cue. "From *The Copper Beeches* . . . and that reminds me. As he was dropping me off, Charles said something about a Holmes story by Conan Doyle I've never read. Do you know what he was talking about?"

"Oh, yes," said Malcolm. "You're not going to believe this. It goes back to the period after Conan Doyle temporarily killed Holmes off. You probably know the dates."

"The story of him and Moriarty allegedly falling into the Reichenbach Falls locked in each other's arms was published in 1893. I can't remember the exact gap, but it was about ten years later that Doyle raised him from the dead. But you still haven't answered the question."

"Prepare yourself for a shock," Malcolm warned him. "Conan Doyle was a close friend of Dr Samuel Carrington, who was Charles's grandfather. They'd met as medical students and he often visited Carwelton Hall. In 1894 he stood godfather to Dr Carrington's son — who later became Charles's father — and his christening present was a brand new Holmes story. Ten copies, privately bound. It's never been published."

"*What?*" Maltravers spluttered as misdirected coffee sent him into a paroxysm of coughing. Malcolm looked amused as he choked, staring at him in disbelief as though he had casually announced he had stumbled across the genuine Van Gogh's *Sunflowers* at a church jumble sale and the Japanese had a twenty-three million pound print hanging on the wall.

"You'd better slap him on the back," he told his wife.

Lucinda stood up and hit Maltravers between the shoulder blades with a blow that would have dented metal.

"Enough!" he gasped. "How many ways do you two want to kill me? Shock or a broken spine?"

He collapsed back in his chair and gulped as he recovered.

"Now let me get this straight," he said finally. "The man who gave me a lift here tonight actually has an unknown Sherlock Holmes story, written by Conan Doyle *himself* for God's sake! That's like saying the *Titanic* has just docked safely at New York!"

"Come on, Gus," Lucinda objected. "It's only a book—and quite a short one at that."

"It's only a book in the same way that Everest is only a large hill," he corrected. "Publishers would kill to get hold of it. It's worth . . . God, you can't put a price on it. Why has it never been published?"

"Conan Doyle didn't want it to be," Malcolm explained. "Charles's grandfather suggested it after he brought Holmes back, but he insisted it was a private gift just for his godson and the family."

"Can Carrington prove its authenticity?"

"Every copy signed by Doyle and volume one containing a handwritten personal message to his godson," Malcolm told him. "Plus the letters the family exchanged with him when they asked him about publication and he insisted it was just for them. Amazing isn't it?"

"It's bloody miraculous," Maltravers said feelingly. "But Doyle died in 1930, so Charles Carrington could only have known him as a child, if he ever met him at all. Why does he still feel bound by something he said nearly a hundred years ago?"

"Charles certainly met Doyle," Malcolm confirmed. "He's shown us a photograph of himself as a toddler sitting on his knee. All he can remember is a very old man with a thick moustache. But as far as he's concerned, Doyle said the book was just for the family and that's all there is to it. Gentleman's word and all that sort of thing."

Maltravers shook his head wonderingly as he stared into the fire, unable to make any adequate comment. The house he had left a couple of hours earlier contained the equivalent in crime fiction of another Mozart symphony or an undiscovered Jane Austen novel.

And its owner was keeping it, not for reasons of possessiveness, but out of respect for the wishes of a man who had been dead more than fifty years; meanwhile, his wife operated on a very different code of behaviour.

Chapter Two

Late autumn had frosted the edges of Cumbria and it would not be long before winter lay snow like nuns' white caps on the tops. Great blocks of bottle green conifers stood amid deciduous trees, their leaves stained all the shades of sherry and beer. Far below where Maltravers leaned against a wooden gate, Windermere reflected bruised clouds still swollen with unfallen rain, its waters a tongue of rough-cut slate along its long hollow in the hills. Away to the west, the peaks of Harrison Stickle and Pike o'Stickle rose mistily above the Langdale valley. The only sound was the faint, trembling bleat of a sheep floating down from the fellside behind him. A newspaper with offices in the noisy and noisome City Road had actually paid him to come here and conduct one of the most entertaining interviews of his life; he decided he would reward it by breaking the first rule of journalism and put in only genuine expenses for the trip.

Maltravers had spent a wonderful morning in the company of Dame Ethel Simister, the outrageous *grande dame* of the English theatre, living out her seventh age in a small hotel, memories unimpaired and wit wicked, who had regaled him with a series of scandalous anecdotes and acid comments. A great many paid no respect to the laws of libel, but there were enough for his piece and several others left over which he would delight in repeating privately. He laughed aloud, recalling one particular story as he watched a kestrel hover on vibrating wings above the field in front of him. There were many worse ways of earning a living. A spurt of wind threw a drift of rain into his face and he went back to his car to return to Brook Cottage. The previous night's problems had been caused, he had been informed, by worn points, an affliction which he thought only inconvenienced ballet dancers.

As he drove away, the kestrel dipped its beak and fell soundlessly and there was a little death in the grass.

They were the last to arrive at Carwelton Hall that evening, Maltravers adding his car to the end of the line of vehicles curved in a semi-circle on the drive in front of the house. Charles Carrington opened the door and led them through to the lounge, where the other guests were already gathered. Maltravers heard Lucinda draw in her breath sharply as they entered the room.

"I think you two know everybody," Carrington said. "But I must introduce . . . Gus isn't it? Fine." He turned to the group sitting round the open fire. "This is Gus Maltravers, the writer I've been telling you about. My partner Stephen Campbell and his wife Sophie, Charlotte Quinn, Alan Morris our local vicar, and Duggie Lydden."

Maltravers instantly understood Lucinda's reaction as Carrington continued. "And this is Geoffrey Howard, an old friend of Jennifer's who has just come back from Nigeria."

Campbell was completely bald and the smooth skin of his face seemed as tightly stretched as the dome of his skull; when he raised his eyebrows, which he did frequently, a grid of deep parallel creases appeared across his forehead. He was dressed rather formally for the occasion, gold links of a watch-chain glinting across his waistcoat. With permed hair carrying a stain of henna and too much rouge on her vulpine face, his wife looked like a barmaid who had married well. Howard was tall and powerfully built with a naval-style full set of black beard and moustache and a crescent of old scar tissue pushing down the flesh over his right eye. The uncollared Reverend Morris was clearly comfortably removed from church-mouse poverty, with Savile Row in every expensive stitch of his suit. His face was long and aesthetic, the eyes narrow and penetrating, pencil lines of hair streaked back from the high forehead. In his early fifties, he looked out of his time, like the younger son of a titled nineteenth-century family who had taken the traditional path of entering the church as a suitable profession for a gentleman rather than from any sense of vocation. Charlotte Quinn was handsome and elegant in a burgundy cocktail dress, black patterned tights and low-heeled patent leather shoes with a glint of gold metal at the heels. Maltravers nodded at them all as he was introduced, then observed Lydden more closely as he sat down.

He appeared an unprepossessing lover, below average height now becoming exaggerated by creeping excess weight, partly disguised by a double breasted pearl grey suit. A vivid green tie clashed hideously with a blue shirt and Maltravers remembered Lucinda saying that his business was not very successful; if that was an example of his colour sense, it was not surprising. The face held some remains of what must have been good looks several years earlier, suggesting cunning rather than intelligence, and the pale ginger hair was combed forward in an attempt to cover its retreat. He seemed perfectly at ease as a dinner guest of one of his mistresses's husbands; Maltravers sourly admired the man's gall, but felt that Jennifer Carrington could have shown better taste. As Carrington handed him his drink, she walked into the room, wearing an apricot dress matched to the flame of her hair. Lydden's eyes flashed at her, briefly but hungrily; catching the look, Maltravers glanced quizzically at Lucinda who pursed her lips in silent cynicism.

"Hello," said Jennifer Carrington. "Everyone's arrived then? Dinner's nearly ready. Finish your drinks and then we'll eat."

She sat down between Maltravers and Geoffrey Howard.

"You look much better than you did last night," she commented. "I hope you've not caught a cold or anything?"

"Not so far," Maltravers replied. "And thank you again for helping me out. I hate to think how much worse it could have become."

"You don't know Geoffrey, do you?" she said. "We met years ago and he just turned up out of the blue." She moved her chair back slightly so that the two men could talk to each other.

"Out of the blue from Nigeria," Maltravers observed.

"Yes, I'm a civil engineer and was working on a dam project," Howard replied. "I only came back a few weeks ago and decided to look up some old friends. Someone told me who Jennifer had married and I rang up and was invited to dinner."

"Have you come far tonight?"

"From just outside Manchester, but it only takes an hour or so on the M6," Howard said. "Charles has been telling us all about you, but I'm afraid I've never read anything you've written. I'm sorry."

"Don't apologise," Maltravers told him. "You're in a majority. I don't do five hundred page sagas with regular outbreaks of bodice ripping, spy fiction or crime, which doesn't leave much of an audience. What's it like building dams in Africa?"

Maltravers gave the appearance of listening to Howard on a subject in which he had neither expertise nor interest, which allowed him the opportunity of examining Lydden again from time to time. Charles Carrington was sitting next to him and, as they talked, Jennifer went to sit on the arm of her husband's chair, resting her hand on his shoulder. Maltravers was wondering if it was a further act of deception or perhaps an oblique message to Lydden that she was tiring of their affair, when he saw Carrington move her hand away without looking at her. There was no reason for it and Jennifer appeared momentarily startled, glancing at her husband with concern before standing up abruptly and announcing that dinner was ready. Maltravers was still thinking about the incident and what, if anything, it might mean as they crossed the hall to the dining-room, high and gracious with the deep brown mirror surface of a long rosewood table catching the lights from a pair of silver four-stemmed candelabra, glittering on silver cutlery set by sage green leather place mats with a coat of arms embossed in gold leaf in the centre. Maltravers had been put between Morris and Charlotte Quinn. She could look back on forty but the figure in the wine-dark dress with a loop of pearls at the neck was still that of a young woman and tousled, deep auburn hair was only faintly touched with cobweb grey. He noticed a wedding-ring, but it was worn on her right hand.

"We've not had a chance to speak," he said as he held the ladderback dining-chair for her. "I remember the name but don't know what you do or anything."

"I run a gift shop in Stricklandgate in Kendal," she replied. "I'm almost embarrassed to say I called it Quintessence."

"Ingenious, but you could have used Quinquereme," Maltravers replied, as he took his place next to her. "Although the apes and peacocks might have caused the odd crisis in the stockroom."

Her laugh was low pitched, in key with her contralto voice. "You're quick and that's very clever. I might use it for the new shop I'm planning in Keswick. Would you mind?"

"Not in the least, I'd be flattered," he replied as she passed him a bowl of grated parmesan. "You sell the usual souvenirs I suppose?"

"Dear God, no," she replied firmly. "There's enough second-rate tat about for the tourists without me adding to it. I leave Lakeland tea-cosies and Wordsworth's wretched 'Daffodils' printed on tea-cloths made in Taiwan to the others. You must call in sometime and see for yourself."

"I'll do that," he promised. "Is it your own business?"

"Yes. After my husband left me, Charles lent me the money to set it up. I'm glad to say I've paid him back now."

Maltravers began to scatter the cheese on his minestrone.

"I guessed you were divorced from the wedding-ring. I've been through that myself, but at least it involved just the two of us. Did you have children?"

He realised he had made a mistake as he casually turned to her again and a spasm of recollected pain flashed across eyes of uncertain colour, like pools of oil. The deep red petals of the lips, which had parted in laughter only moments before, stiffened as though she was controlling herself.

"Both my children died of a congenital heart disease before they were twelve," she said. "My husband went off with someone I thought was a friend three months after our daughter's funeral."

"Oh, Christ." Maltravers looked apologetic. "I'm sorry. That was very clumsy of me."

"You weren't to know," she told him. "I'm afraid you caught me off guard with a lot of defences down. I'm usually more careful when strangers ask me things like that because I know how much it can embarrass them."

She touched his arm with a gesture of forgiveness. "Anyway it was a long time ago now, and I'd rather have had my children and lost them than never had them at all."

Maltravers could think of nothing to say that did not sound either patronising or meaningless, then the moment between them was broken by an incongruous outburst of laughter from the other end of the table.

"Gus has a much better one than that," Malcolm was saying. "Tell them about that MP you interviewed once. The one with the talking parrot."

For a while conversation around the table became general then settled down into smaller groups again and Maltravers started talking to Alan Morris. Urbane and cultivated company as a dinner guest, the widowed vicar of Attwater was obviously not inclined to throw open his vestry to the poor. If the Church of England was indeed the Tory party at prayer, Morris would be the perfect cleric to preach the sermon, assuring them that a rich man could enter the kingdom of Heaven with no difficulty, despite the founder's warnings to the contrary. His conversation was highly secular and, when the subject turned to literature, displayed a familiarity with books whose contents bishops are expected to deplore. Maltravers, who had no illusions about Holy Orders producing automatic Becket-style conversions, felt that if he had been following his calling around the time Carwelton Hall was built, Morris would have been a classic pluralist and very worldly agent for the Almighty. He finally abandoned his entertaining company to talk to Charlotte Quinn again.

"I understand Duggie Lydden has a shop in Kendal as well," he said. "Anywhere near yours?"

"Two doors away," she replied and he was struck by the undisguised hostility in her voice. "At least it was still there when I set out this evening. I expect it to go bust any time. When you look at that shirt and tie, what can you expect?"

"It is a rather eccentric colour combination," Maltravers agreed, intrigued by her instantly revealed animosity. "Do I gather you're . . . not exactly the best of friends?"

"I wouldn't spit in Duggie Lydden's mouth if his teeth were on fire," she said, the startling bluntness accompanied by a bland smile. "Does that answer your question?"

"I think I grasp the general drift," Maltravers replied evenly. "I seem to be saying all the wrong things to you, don't I?"

"Don't worry. I've reached the stage in life where I don't care what I say or what anyone thinks about it. It shocks some people, but you look as though you can handle it." She smiled apologetically. "No, I'm sorry. I've had one drink too many tonight and some things have come too near the surface."

Maltravers caught her distasteful glance towards Jennifer Carrington.

"I'm being rather slow, aren't I?" he commented mildly. "How long has Charles been a friend of yours?"

One eyebrow arched as Charlotte Quinn gave him an appreciative but warning look.

"Now that's being too clever. You're so sharp, you'll cut yourself, as my grandmother used to say."

"Not all that clever," he contradicted. "You're not making much of an effort to put a polite face on certain things."

It had not taken any particular brilliance for him to reach obvious conclusions about Charlotte Quinn's feelings. He was about to say something else when Carrington stood up and spoke to his wife.

"Geoffrey has asked to see round the house," he said. "Can you take everyone else back to the lounge for coffee? Unless anybody else would like the guided tour?"

"Actually, I've never seen the Hall properly," said Malcolm.

"Perhaps you'd like to join us," Carrington said to Maltravers. "There's something in the library you'll certainly want to see."

Duggie Lydden and the Reverend Morris stayed with them, but Campbell and his wife went with the other three women as Carrington began to escort them through his family home. Rebuilt in the nineteenth century, but with roots going back to the Restoration, the house was a fine example of its period, but Maltravers had little taste for Victorian style. Its unremitting ponderousness always struck him as the product of the highly righteous and privileged section of a society convinced that God was an Englishman who would let his chosen people rule the world for ever and they should accordingly build their homes and furniture like their monuments, solid, uncompromising and permanent. He took only polite interest in what Carrington showed them — which was more than Lydden did — while Howard seemed endlessly fascinated and well informed and Malcolm and Morris made intelligent comments. But Maltravers's interest rose considerably when he heard Carrington mention the library as they went downstairs and he followed the others through another door off the hall. Hurrying to catch up, Maltravers banged his head painfully on the top of the lintel as he entered the room.

"Sorry, I should have warned you," Carrington apologised. "That door's ridiculously low. However, this will take your mind off it."

He crossed to what appeared to be a cupboard next to one of the bookcases, but behind the wooden door was a wall safe with a combination lock. Carrington operated the dial then pulled it open and Maltravers could see that it contained a pile of identical books and some papers. Carrington took out one of the slender volumes and turned to offer it to him.

"Here you are," he said with a smile. Maltravers accepted it and read the title embossed in gold leaf on the leather spine: *The Attwater Firewitch*. Underneath was Arthur Conan Doyle's name and the Roman numeral I. Opening it with almost reverential care, he read the fading ink of the handwritten inscription on the flyleaf: 'For my godson, William Redmond Carrington, on the occasion of his Christening, December 18th, 1894. From his most affectionate godfather, in the hope that in later years he will enjoy reading the final adventure of Sherlock Holmes and Dr John Watson.' Underneath was Conan Doyle's signature. Maltravers turned another page and saw the title of the first chapter — AN ENCOUNTER AT BUSHELLS — then closed the volume reluctantly but firmly.

"I'm very tempted to start reading and then I wouldn't want to stop," he said, offering the book back. "But thank you for letting me see it. I can still hardly believe the story of how you come to have it. Malcolm explained it all last night."

"I wouldn't be so unkind as to let you do no more than just see it."
Carrington took the book and returned it to the safe. "From what
Malcolm's told me about your enthusiasm for detective fiction, that
would be unforgiveable. I'll lend you the photocopy I've made of the
text, although I'm afraid I can't do that immediately. There's only
the one copy and it's with a great Sherlockian at the moment, but I'm
expecting it back in a day or so. All I ask is that you return it before
you leave or send it back by registered post."

Maltravers frowned at him. "You lend out a copy? Somebody
could go off to a publisher with it."

"I'm careful who I lend it to," Carrington replied. "And I'm sure I
can trust you as much as the others. Anyway, without the letters
from Conan Doyle, which are also in the safe, it could be nothing
more than a clever pastiche, so nobody can get away with anything."

Morris, who was standing next to Maltravers, nudged him.

"Believe me, you'll enjoy it," he said. "I'm another of the chosen
few who've read it. You have as well, haven't you Duggie?"

"What?" Lydden turned from leafing through a book he had
taken from the shelf on the opposite side of the room. "Oh, yes, it's
quite good."

"Quite good," Carrington echoed slightly caustically, then
smiled at Maltravers before joining Malcolm and Geoffrey Howard
who were examining a set of water-colours of Borrowdale above the
mantelpiece as Jennifer Carrington walked into the room.

"Your coffee's going to be stone cold," she said. "Haven't you
finished yet?"

"We're just coming," Carrington replied, but Maltravers saw he
was not looking at his wife. The instant she had appeared he had
turned straight towards Lydden. "This is, if Duggie can tear himself
away from that book."

"What?" Lydden appeared startled. "Oh, yes. It's just some
poetry by a chap called Herrick. He was one of the Lake poets wasn't
he?"

"Hardly," corrected Carrington. "Two centuries earlier."

"Never been keen on poetry anyway," Lydden said indifferently, replacing the book on the shelf. "I just thought he was
local."

Maltravers inwardly despaired at another manifestation of the average Englishman's ignorance of his literary heritage, but was much more interested in Carrington's reaction when Jennifer had appeared. Coupled with the incident before dinner, he was now certain that Carrington was not as unaware about what was going on as Lydden — and perhaps his wife — believed. Lydden had not looked round until Carrington had spoken to him, so he might not have noticed anything, but Jennifer could hardly have missed it. She had turned and walked out of the room almost the moment Carrington had spoken. Maltravers wondered whose idea it had been that Lydden should be among the guests. If Carrington himself had suggested it, perhaps he had done so to give himself an opportunity of confirming something he suspected. And he would not do that unless he intended acting on any evidence; Maltravers wondered what he would do if he ever had proof.

Back in the lounge, Lucinda and Charlotte looked relieved as the rest of the party rejoined them. Campbell was telling some faintly funny and lengthy legal story which he obviously thought hilarious; his wife's face was set in the fixed smile of a mother listening to her child performing their inadequate party piece on the piano.

"Did Charles show you the famous Sherlock Holmes book?" Jennifer asked Maltravers as she handed him his coffee. "I expect I really ought to read it myself sometime."

"Haven't you done that already?"

"I keep suggesting it, but she's not interested." Carrington, who was sitting next to Maltravers, smiled rather patronisingly at his wife. "Jennifer's passion is for incredibly long historical romances."

"Well, putting aside its literary value, it's almost certainly the most valuable thing your husband owns," Maltravers told her, then turned to Carrington. "You won't allow it to be published even now?"

Carrington shook his head firmly. "Not under any circumstances. Conan Doyle didn't want it to be and that's all there is to it."

"No matter how much you were offered?" asked Maltravers. "They say that every man has his price."

"That depends on what you're trying to buy," Carrington replied simply. "Or at least it should."

In a world which judged everything by its potential monetary value, where people were constantly ready to ditch moral obligations or betray personal confidences to make a fast and sordid buck, Carrington's attitude would be considered risible, but Maltravers found it reassuring that some people could still not be bought.

"Then what about its literary importance?" he pursued. "You're denying millions the pleasure of reading it. That seems very selfish."

Carrington shrugged. "Then Conan Doyle was selfish and there's nothing I can do about it. You're not the first to try that argument, Gus, but it won't change my mind."

"And what happens when you die?" Maltravers added. "What guarantee have you got that whoever inherits it will have your . . . moral squint?"

Carrington hesitated, as though deciding whether to say something.

"I've made certain arrangements about that," he said finally, then smiled. "Any more questions, Mr Journalist?"

"Only an occasional journalist now," Maltravers corrected. "But bad habits die hard. If I was still a reporter, I'd be looking for an angle on how secure your safe is in the circumstances."

"Four figure combination with the standard hundred numbers on the dial," Carrington replied. "Which gives a hundred million permutations if anybody wants to try and find it by chance. If they get it wrong too often, an alarm sounds in the offices of the firm I bought it from, who would call the police. I'm the only one who knows the right numbers."

"Duress signal?" Maltravers enquired. Carrington looked impressed.

"Yes — not many people know about those."

"I only do because a disgustingly rich friend of mine in London has a safe with one. He suggested I should have one fitted, but then the most valuable thing in my house would be the safe. Hardly worth it really."

"It is in this case." Carrington stood up. "Excuse me, but I've forgotten the liqueurs."

Maltravers watched him cross to the drinks cabinet, asking everyone what they would like. Presumably, with both his children dead, Jennifer would inherit the books; her track record of faithfulness did not suggest she would have any compunction about selling to the highest bidder. Did Carrington's 'certain arrangements' take care of that? Maltravers's eyes went casually back to Jennifer, now talking animatedly to Lucinda and Morris; Howard and Lydden were in conversation with the Campbells and Malcolm was flicking through a copy of *Country Life* he had taken from the magazine rack by his chair. It was a perfectly normal after-dinner scene, but one which decently ignored the fact that their hostess was an adulteress, a social solecism overlooked because it was bad manners to draw attention to it. Previous generations did not discuss certain things in front of the children or the servants; for all their outspokenness, their modern descendants were not greatly different.

It was turned midnight when they left, skeins of stars bright and cold as the gathering frost glittering like diamond fragments scattered in soot. Smoke from roaring exhausts billowed yellow in the glare of headlamps as they scraped a crust of ice from car windows and shouted good-night to each other. Campbell waved to Howard, Morris and Maltravers to back up so that he could negotiate round Lydden's car which was parked in front of his, then they all moved towards the gates.

"Executrix," Maltravers murmured as he pulled away.

"What?" said Malcolm.

"Nothing important. Just something I was trying to work out." He glanced at Lydden's car as he drove past it. "It looks as though Duggie's been invited to stay for a nightcap. Interesting."

"He must be . . ." Lucinda turned round to look through the rear window, but the front door of Carwelton Hall was closed. "No, he's not coming. What's going on?"

Maltravers turned left on to the main road, following the others. "I spied with my little eye something beginning with S. Suspicion. And if turns into C for certainty it could become D for divorce. O for and done with. Sorry about that."

"Do you mean Charles knows?" asked Malcolm.

"He's getting there I think — which is more than Campbell and Howard are incidentally. Why are they going this way? The motorway's in the other direction."

"Turning right out of Carwelton Hall on that blind bend can be fatal," Malcolm explained. "You go left and turn round in the lay-by just up here. There they go."

Maltravers flashed his lights at the two cars as they and Morris passed them.

"It also seems that Duggie was the first to arrive this evening," he added. "His car was parked at the front of the queue. Revealing comment on modern etiquette. Screw the wife, then turn up early so the husband can serve you what we might call cuckold's gin."

"Duggie Lydden's a conceited pig," Lucinda said bluntly. "Tonight was just the sort of thing that would appeal to his warped sense of humour."

"Well he and Jennifer may soon have to stop laughing," Maltravers commented. "I also had an interesting chat with Charlotte Quinn. What do you know about her?"

"Ah, that's quite another story." Lucinda leaned forward from the back seat to talk to him. "Things would have been very different for Charles if she'd had her way."

"That I'd worked out. He could have saved himself a lot of grief if he'd married that lady. What went wrong?"

Jennifer Carrington leaned over the banisters half-way down the stairs trying to hear the conversation in the library, but the door was closed. She thought of standing outside the door, but would look foolish if it was unexpectedly opened. Carrington had suggested she should go to bed while he and Duggie Lydden talked about business. Frustrated, she went back upstairs and lay fully dressed on the bed, staring at the ceiling.

Downstairs, Lydden watched Carrington guardedly as he poured him another drink. The request to stay as the others left had been made discreetly but with an air of anticipated acceptance. Jennifer had shrugged at him behind her husband's back, indicating that she was as mystified as he was. As he waited for Carrington to speak, Lydden remained as calm as he could.

"It's about the shop, Duggie," Carrington said as he handed him the glass. He had not poured one for himself. "The bank's been on to me."

Lydden maintained his impassiveness as he accepted the gin and tonic, but felt instantly alert and defensive.

"Business is quite good," he said casually. "What's the problem?"

"Repayment of the loan." Carrington sat down behind his desk. "You've cancelled your standing order."

"Oh, that was just a temporary thing because of a cash flow problem," Lydden protested. "There's no real difficulty."

"Nothing has been paid for six months." Carrington gazed at him across the flame of his gold lighter as he lit a thin cigar. "The bank advised me after three and I told them to let me know if it reached this stage. That doesn't sound like a temporary cash flow problem."

"Six months?" Lydden covered his sense of being trapped with a tone of disbelief. "That's ridiculous. I wrote to the bank after only a month to tell them to start it again. They can't have received my letter."

"And you didn't notice the repayments hadn't restarted when you did your books?" Carrington left a silence after the observation, examining the glowing end of the cigar. "However, I'm afraid I must ask for the full arrears to be cleared immediately and normal repayments reinstated. I'm sorry, Duggie."

"What do you mean by immediately?"

"By the end of this month at the latest."

Lydden shifted uncomfortably in his chair. Being faced by an outraged husband would have been considerably easier to deal with.

"Well, I'll do my best," he said evasively. "It could be a bit of a stretch though."

"Really?" Carrington said mildly. "You just told me things were going well. Anyway, I'm sure you don't want to put me in a position where I have to send the receivers in. I'm quite entitled to do that under the terms of our agreement. The bank has already suggested it, but we've been friends a long time Duggie and . . . well, fellow Masons always do the right thing by each other don't they?"

Lydden's discomfort grew as Carrington looked at him very directly.

"I'll sort it out," he said. "Don't worry." Without thinking what he was doing, he finished his drink too quickly.

"I've got nothing to worry about," Carrington stood up. "At least not about business matters. Sorry to end the evening like this, but I wanted to raise it as soon as possible. I'll see you out . . . Jennifer will be wondering what's keeping me."

As he drove away, Lydden's mind raced. This was not just a matter of hastily retreating from another affair. Jennifer Carrington meant more than casual sex, she could provide the answer to certain problems. It was a dangerous answer, but Carrington's demands for repayment moved them from the urgent to the critical. He would have to talk to her.

Jennifer Carrington breathed deeply as she heard Lydden's wheels spin violently on the gravel drive and her husband come upstairs. She had undressed, sprayed herself with cologne and put on a pair of Chinese-style pyjamas. When Carrington walked in, she smiled brilliantly.

"What on earth have you two been talking about, darling?" she asked. "I thought you were never coming to bed."

Several buttons running down from the Mandarin collar of the silk jacket were unfastened and a curve of soft flesh was provocatively visible beneath the material's sheen of jet with its fiery pattern of jacaranda flowers.

"Just something I wanted to straighten out." He walked towards the adjacent dressing-room. "Nothing important."

As she listened to him through the half-open door, undressing and cleaning his teeth, Jennifer Carrington took off the jacket and left it sprawled across the bed then pulled the duvet up to her chin. Carrington showed no reaction when he reappeared and climbed in beside her, switching off his bedside light. After a few moments, she slithered towards him, an affectionate, suggestive purr at the back of her throat.

"Sorry, darling, do you mind? I'm rather tired."

He turned away and Jennifer Carrington stared at his back in dismay. It was the first time he had ever refused to make love to her. She was suddenly afraid that she was losing control.

Chapter Three

Five minutes after Charles Carrington left for work the next morning, the telephone rang in Carwelton Hall and Jennifer leapt at it.

"Thank God! I was just going to call you," she said. "Charles knows what's going on."

"Are you certain? Has he said anything to you?"

"He doesn't need to. I *know*. Believe me."

"Might he do anything before Thursday?"

"Perhaps, but we can't move until then can we?" There was a note of panic in her voice.

"Of course we can't, but it's only a couple of days. Call me if anything happens, but otherwise I'll see you then. And keep calm."

"Will you come and see me before?" She sounded pleading.

"No. Charles could be having you watched. Just hang on."

"All right." She sobbed suddenly. "Christ, I never thought it would be this bad. I'm terrified."

"Stop panicking, I'll look after you. You always did need an older man. It's going to work."

In Brook Cottage, Maltravers wrote up his piece for the *Independent*, saving the Features Editor several tricky decisions by omitting certain stories which would have caused a number of actors to start screaming dramatically for their lawyers. Malcolm was at work and Lucinda out teaching, so when he finished he drove into Kendal to post his copy and have lunch. He parked in the market square opposite the old Working Men's Institute, now rather inappropriately painted pink and white, then walked down

37

Stricklandgate to the main post office. As he made his way back up the hill, looking for somewhere to eat, he found he was passing Quintessence and examined the window. Charlotte Quinn's comments about her stock had been right. What he could see included elegant wooden and silver ornaments, first-class porcelain — thankfully not crafted into impossibly perfect animals, winsome children or nauseatingly lovable tramps — fine woollens and striking fabrics. The shop would have graced Covent Garden, but the prices were considerably less than those demanded and paid in WC2. An old-style shop bell suspended from a curve of sprung metal tinkled as he opened the door and moments later Charlotte Quinn appeared from the back of the premises.

"I'm sorry, but we're just . . ." She stopped as she recognised him. "Oh, hello again. I'm afraid I was about to close for lunch. But if you've already decided on something I can let you have it."

"No, I was just going to browse," he said. "It's the sort of place I ought to bring Tess to. She's the one with the real taste. I just supply the money."

"Your wife?" she queried.

"Not yet, but she's working on it," he replied with a grin. "I only escaped last Leap Year by being out of the country on the twenty-ninth of February. She's the actress Tess Davy. She's due here at the weekend after the play she's in ends its provincial tour in Chester. Then she's got a free week before they start rehearsals for London. I'll come back with her. Anyway, let me buy you lunch. I assume you know a decent place."

"I usually go to the Wheatsheaf just across the road," she said. "Their menu plays havoc with the diet but what the hell? All right, thank you. I'll be with you in a moment. Turn the sign on the door to Closed, will you?"

He examined a rack of silk ties while he waited, then they left the shop and crossed over Stricklandgate and into the pub. They were just ahead of the lunchtime rush and managed to find themselves a table by the window overlooking the busy main street.

"According to the book of conversational gambits, I should ask if you enjoyed yourself last night," Maltravers commented as he returned from the bar with their food and drinks. "However, I

38

think that would be as tactless as asking Mrs Kennedy if she liked her day in Dallas."

"Something like that," Charlotte Quinn agreed. "It was loathsome, but I'll curb my tongue. Coming from the south, you're not used to people speaking their minds."

"I lived in Manchester for more than a year, so I know something about northern bluntness," he replied. "And I think you were offended by . . . the presence of one guest in particular and his connection — how's that for polite Home Counties euphemism? — with our hostess?"

She laughed. "Oh, very circumspect — I said last night you were too clever. You pick things up very quickly. How much do you know about what's going on there?"

"Lucinda and Malcolm have told me a good deal," he admitted. "I know that Jennifer Carrington and Duggie Lydden are having an affair . . . and something about yourself and Charles."

"Yes, but you don't know all of it." Maltravers followed her gaze out of the window to where a shop with Lakeland Interiors above the window stood on the opposite side of the road next door but one to her own. Charlotte Quinn kept looking at it as she continued.

"Three years ago that place nearly went to the wall. The bank was about to foreclose when Duggie Lydden went crawling to Charles for help. They knew each other through the Masons but they go back further than that. Charles put up twenty thousand pounds and saved him. Duggie has paid very little of it back. And how does the little sod show his gratitude? By screwing his wife and then going to his house to laugh in his face in front of his friends." She turned back to Maltravers. "Any more questions?"

"Why did you accept the invitation?"

"I've known Charles an awfully long time and, dear God, I've done my best to accept Jennifer, despite what I think of her," she said. "I've kept going to Carwelton Hall since the marriage because of my feelings for him. But I didn't know Duggie was going to be there last night. I don't know how I controlled myself."

"You did it very well," Maltravers assured her. "And from what I've been told, Jennifer is just one of a small crowd. It seems that any woman who isn't green with two heads has a chance with Duggie."

"That's about it," Charlotte confirmed. "He made a play for me once, but I made it quite clear that I wasn't going to join his collection of easy lays. By the time I'd finished, I'd verbally castrated the randy little bugger."

Maltravers felt certain that Charlotte Quinn's acid tongue would have made a comprehensive job of the operation.

"How long have you known Charles?" he added.

"Nearly twenty years. When I was married, we all used to go on holiday together. I remember how he nursed Margaret while she died of cancer by inches. Christ, that was terrible. Then David was killed and Gillian was destroyed by drugs — do you know anything about all this?"

"Yes," he said. "Charles seems to have been a very unfortunate man."

"And it's still happening to him," she said bitterly. "Jennifer set out to get him and nothing could stop her. He was dreadfully vulnerable and didn't stand a chance. Some of us tried to warn him, but he was besotted. It's the most stupid thing he's ever done."

She finished her wine at one swallow. "Can I have another please? No, I'll pay if you'll collect them. Here you are."

She took a purse from her handbag and gave Maltravers the money. While he was waiting at the bar to be served, he decided he may as well probe her feelings further; she was obviously in the mood to talk.

"As far as I can work it out, there must have been about ten years between Charles's wife dying and when he met Jennifer," he said as he sat down again. "Were you divorced at that time?"

"I was divorced in 1975." She sighed wearily. "And yes, that's what really hurts. You don't have to be a genius to work that out. I loved him very much — I still love him — but somehow I just couldn't . . . I don't know. I just messed it all up."

They had finished their meal and she accepted a cigarette when he offered his packet, looking at her thoughtfully.

"Why are you telling me all this?" he asked. "This is only the second time we've met and you're pouring out your life story."

She exhaled smoke slowly, as though trying to explain it to herself.

40

"Last night I wanted to scream," she said finally. "What was happening in that house was sick and I had to go through the pretence of behaving as though nothing was wrong. It's been building up inside me all morning and my assistant's off today so there was nobody I could talk to. If I hadn't met you, I'd probably have blurted it all out to some customer in the shop. Sorry to use you like a member of the Samaritans. I only hope I've got it right that I can trust you."

"Completely," Maltravers assured her. "None of this will go any further. I'm glad we bumped into each other." He paused for a moment. "Charles may have been stupid over Jennifer, but he's still an intelligent man. Do you think he knows about the affair — or at least suspects something?"

She shrugged as she stubbed out the hardly smoked cigarette. "I often wonder about that. He's never said anything to me to indicate that he does, but I can't believe he could be so unaware — although there's no fool like an old fool is there?"

"Stop putting him down," Maltravers told her. "He deserves better than that from you. I think he may at least have guessed about Lydden, but if he hasn't then somebody who says they care for him ought to tell him instead of carrying a torch and wallowing in their own misery."

Charlotte Quinn's face flashed angrily, then she looked remorseful.

"Ouch," she said. "That hurt. You did learn to call a spade a spade in the north didn't you? You're quite right of course, but I've been through that hoop lots of times. I persuade myself that I don't want to hurt him, then my conscience tells me that I'm deceiving him as well by staying quiet. But perhaps it's really because I don't trust my own motives. If I break up the marriage, am I doing it for him or me? Shakespeare said that conscience makes cowards of us all."

"In the occasional gaps in an active sex life, Shakespeare managed to say something about virtually everything," commented Maltravers. "But I don't think deathless verse is of much help at the moment. None of this is my business, but you should talk to him. Whether he suspects or not, you can't lose anything and it's the least he deserves from you."

"Perhaps." Charlotte Quinn shrugged in indecision then smiled apologetically. "And you just came into town for a quiet lunch, not to have some inadequate woman unburden her soul to you. Sorry."

"Now you're knocking yourself," he said. "Don't. You're not inadequate."

"Aren't I?" she replied cynically. "Tell me about it. If I'm not inadequate, how did I lose a husband and then fail to get the one man I wanted and could have made happy? Let's face it, Gus, I was seen off by another woman and a much younger one at that. I must be very stupid."

"No," Maltravers corrected. "Charles may have been stupid — in fact it looks very much as if he was — but that wasn't your fault."

"I'd like to think that." Charlotte Quinn appeared unconvinced as she stood up. "Thanks for lunch and for listening, but I must get back."

They parted outside the pub with Maltravers promising to return to Quintessence with Tess. He watched Charlotte Quinn cross Stricklandgate and unlock the shop door then went back to his car and drove out into the Langdale Valley. He parked by the pub at the foot of Stickle Ghyll and walked up the rough path of boulders laid alongside the beck as it tumbled down in a series of bubbling, foaming waterfalls from the tarn in the hills. Drained now of all rain, the sky was a translucent autumn blue with drifting meringue clouds casting slow-moving shadows over the wide plain of the valley and the air was clean and cold. As he sat on a rock by crashing white water, Maltravers thought about the dinner party. It might not need Charlotte, or anyone else, to talk to Charles Carrington; if the odd incidents he had noticed really meant anything, the situation at Carwelton Hall would resolve itself one way or another.

"Is anything the matter, darling?" Jennifer Carrington put the question cautiously as her husband sat opposite her reading the paper that evening.

"Should there be?" The paper was not lowered as he replied, but she instinctively knew he was listening to her carefully.

"No, you just seemed a bit . . . distracted," she said. "I thought something might be on your mind and we could talk about it."

The newspaper rustled as Carrington turned the page but remained behind it.

"Nothing for you to worry about."

In the silence that followed the dismissive reply she returned her attention to the television, watching its images without seeing or listening. Duggie had told her about the conversation the previous evening and she felt nervous. Carrington's rejection of her in bed, now coupled with his obvious determination not to talk to her, had destroyed her confidence that she could always mould him the way she wanted. And that was something she had to keep doing. She had to stay calm while she completed the last stages of her part in his murder. She realised that she had finally used the word in her mind; before it had always been 'dealing with Charles' or just 'doing it'. Now that she had grasped the proper word herself, it somehow seemed less terrifying, an acceptance of the inevitability of what had been planned.

"I'm going shopping in Manchester on Thursday," she said casually. "I could try in Sherratt & Hughes for that Kingsley Amis novel you want."

She felt relieved as he folded the paper and finally looked at her.

"Thank you. I never seem to have time to get it in Lancaster. Are you spending the whole day in town?"

"Probably," she replied. "What time will you be back from Carlisle?"

"Midnight at the latest. The meeting should be over about ten."

"Then I'll probably call and see Angela before coming back, but I'll be home before you. I'll wait up."

"There's no need. Excuse me, there are some papers I must look at."

As he walked out of the room, Jennifer Carrington became apprehensive again. The tone of his voice belonged to the office, not to their home and their life together. She stood up and turned off the television then stood in front of the fire, arms folded defensively across her chest as she thought. However strong Charles's suspicions about Duggie were — and everything pointed to them being very strong indeed — it was still all right as long as he didn't come straight out with it. And in two days, he would not be able to do anything.

In the library, Carrington unlocked his briefcase and took out several pages of notes in his precise handwriting. A lifetime as a lawyer had ingrained the practice of putting everything into words on paper. He still had the diary he had kept when his first wife was dying; now, for very different reasons, he was doing the same thing with Jennifer. But the language of the law was detached and unemotional, helpless to capture love, unable to embrace grief, too controlled to express fear. And the rule of the law demanded proof before anyone was guilty. Until that proof came — and he knew that he kept putting off pursuing it — then Jennifer had to be innocent. The law said so.

Duggie Lydden violently punched the buttons on his calculator again to see if entering the figures in a different permutation would somehow miraculously conjure up a less horrendous answer. When the same result inevitably appeared, he swore and looked resignedly at the account books spread across his desk in the office at the back of his shop. The disastrous five numbers were only black on the calculator's display; his bank manager would regard them as being in the deepest red.

Among the documents was his latest credit card demand which included the bill for a hotel in York. Adding on the entry for the necklace he had bought as well, he reckoned the weekend had cost him over a hundred pounds for each time he had coupled with the highly co-operative student from the wine bar. Her insatiable enthusiasm and sexual inventiveness appeared to have been a very costly indulgence; her suggestion that she now thought she might be pregnant was all he had needed. The choice between mainten-ance or the cost of an abortion was academic; he could afford neither. His best hope there was suggesting that someone else was the father. He kept crudely telling other customers in the wine bar that more men had been up her than Helvellyn.

Lydden picked up his latest statement to check what he already knew; the chances of repaying Carrington by the end of the month were non-existent. At his last tetchily polite meeting with the bank manager, the spurious promise of an anticipated contract for refurbishing a cottage in Grasmere bought by a Kensington yuppie as a second home had postponed certain consequences. Now that his over-priced tender had been rejected, there were no delaying tactics left. He was trapped between a grossly exceeded overdraft arrangement and Carrington's ultimatum.

He pushed the papers away peevishly and again wondered about the unspoken but palpable motives behind Carrington's conversation with him after dinner. Having the power to bankrupt your wife's lover would be an attractive situation to any husband. But the answer could now be within his reach. When he had spoken to Jennifer on the phone that morning, she had appeared less unwilling than before to go along with the plan; at least she had said she would think about it. Lydden had always been convinced that a woman ready and willing to start playing around only months after her wedding-day was not going to care overmuch about what else she did to her ageing and malleable husband. And if they succeeded there would be no problems — apart from the minor matter of then getting rid of her. The number of women who could be deceived with a constant stream of facile promises had long since ceased to surprise him. As he thought, the telephone on his desk rang.

"Duggie? When are you coming? I told you Ivor is due back from Sweden tomorrow. I was expecting you hours ago."

"Sorry, got held up by something. I'm on my way."

Lydden rang off, put away the books and turned off the lamp before going out through the back door of Lakeland Interiors into the small walled courtyard where he parked his car. He stopped at an off-licence for a bottle of wine then drove out of Kendal towards Windermere and an isolated, exclusive house set in the hills. Three on the go at the same time, he reflected; it was certainly a personal best.

In her flat above Quintessence, Charlotte Quinn sat in an Edwardian rocking chair, unconsciously stroking the Persian cat on her lap. The room was lit by only a standard lamp as she listened to Sondheim on the record player, a song by an older man deluding himself as he desperately tried to defend his hollow marriage to a much younger wife. One line — Her youth is a sort of present, whatever the price — reminded her of Noël Coward's observation about the potency of cheap music. Her mind went back over the time when she had visited Carwelton Hall every day, watching Charles Carrington grow old and broken as the disease had remorselessly gnawed Margaret's body to a pitiful skeleton wrapped in parchment skin. A few days before her death, she had beckoned Charlotte to bend down and catch her weak and straining voice.

"Make him happy for me please, Charlotte," she had whispered. "I know you love him. Promise."

Slow tears ran down Charlotte's face as she remembered what had happened to the children afterwards and how Charles had turned inward upon himself and she had been unable to reach him. Then, when so much time had passed that she had thought it would never happen, the new wife had appeared. But she had not been an older, mature woman, but an excited girl, over-eager to please Charles's friends with assurances that she really loved him and only wanted to bring him happiness. And now — the tears changed to a scowl of disgust — she laughed at him behind his back with Duggie Lydden.

The record had moved on and now a woman sang about sending in the clowns, Sondheim's brilliant portrayal of confused lovers as painted fools. There was nothing cheap about this music, it was real and cruel and intolerably agonising. Agitatedly, Charlotte Quinn pushed the cat off her lap and crossed the room. There was a harsh scratch as she pulled the needle off, then she went to the window, leaning her forehead against the cool glass, the pane straining with the pressure. Since her spontaneous outpouring to Maltravers over lunch, she had been constantly tormented by his suggestion that she was one of the few people who could tell Charles the truth, however much she dreaded doing it.

Maltravers poured his own gin and peered into the empty cold bucket in the drinks cupboard.

"I'm just going out to get some ice," he murmured, walking towards the kitchen. "I may be some time."

Lucinda looked puzzled as Malcolm laughed then she grasped it for herself.

"Very good, Gus," she called after him. "Original or stolen?"

"Not only original, but just used for the first time," he said as he reappeared. "I've been saving it for the right occasion and, remember, you were there."

He stretched out on the chesterfield, long legs protruding over one of the arms. "I had lunch in Kendal with Charlotte Quinn today and ended up suggesting she spoke to Charles about Duggie and Jennifer. She was just waiting for someone to tell her to do it and I happened to be in the neighbourhood."

"It's a good job you were. Charles is a friend of ours and we've been deceiving him as well by not saying anything." Lucinda put in the last stitch and bit through the cotton, holding up the results to examine it. "That's been worrying me. Do you think she'll do it?"

"Yes," said Maltravers. "Not perhaps for a while, but she'll tell him all right. You know him better than I do. How will he react?"

"He's very correct and disciplined," Lucinda replied. "He won't break down or start being insanely jealous, he'll just do whatever's necessary to sort it out."

"Will he try to save the marriage?"

"No," Lucinda said positively. "Jennifer peeled away a lot of layers he'd built up around himself after everything that had happened. He trusted her enough to let her remove his protection and he could never forgive her for hurting him again. We've always known if this business about Duggie Lydden ever came out, Jennifer would have no way back."

"And she must know that as well," Malcolm added. "Which is something to think about. She starts an affair with the most overworked sex maniac in Cumbria and is bloody careless about disguising the fact. Makes a perverted sort of sense doesn't it?"

"It certainly does, Ollie," Maltravers agreed. "She deliberately wrecks the marriage, and admitting adultery doesn't make people cross you off their invitation lists these days. If it did, the newspaper social columnists would be queuing up for the dole.

Then she screws Charles — in a different sort of way — for a great deal, possibly even half the value of the house. Who's a clever girl then?"

"Are you two serious?" Lucinda demanded.

"Why not?" asked Maltravers. "Marriage laws are ideal for fortune hunters these days. For better, for worse, in sickness and in health till alimony do us part, when I will be richer and you will certainly be poorer. I'm surprised it doesn't happen more often. Perhaps it does."

"Why doesn't she just wait for Charles to die? She could have everything then."

"Half what Charles is worth today is enough and probably preferable to waiting — what? ten years or more? — for the other half," said Maltravers. "Jennifer doesn't strike me as the patient type. She wants it now please — and I don't think she's bothered about how she gets it."

Chapter Four

A pale sun had just risen on Thursday morning as Maltravers worked on Malcolm's word processor — conveniently compatible with his own — completing the final draft of his last act. He had started early and was the only one in the house who was up when the front doorbell rang. Charles Carrington was standing in the porch holding an envelope.

"I saw you through the window, so I can give this to you personally," he said. "It arrived back yesterday."

"The Sherlock Holmes?" Maltravers looked delighted as Carrington handed him the envelope. "You didn't need to bring it round at this hour of the morning."

"I thought I'd make a detour on my way to the office," Carrington explained. "Jennifer's spending the day shopping in Manchester or she'd have dropped it in."

"Thank you very much," Maltravers said. "I should finish writing this morning, so I'll keep Conan Doyle as a treat for later on. Don't worry, it will be perfectly safe."

"I know it will," said Carrington. "I'll be interested in what you think about it. Anyway, I must be off. I want to get to work early because I'm leaving this afternoon to get ready for a meeting. Goodbye."

"By the way," Maltravers added as Carrington turned back towards his car. "I had lunch with Charlotte Quinn in Kendal the other day. She's a very nice lady."

"Charlotte?" Carrington looked slightly reflective. "Yes she is, isn't she? She's been a very good friend to me."

He momentarily juggled his car keys in his hand then smiled slightly and walked to his car without another word. Maltravers watched him drive away then stepped back into the cottage and closed the door.

"You let something show there, Charles," he murmured to himself. "You're having regrets, aren't you?"

Half an hour later, Jennifer Carrington drove out of Carwelton Hall towards the M6, stopping for petrol at the village filling station.

"Where are you off to then, Mrs Carrington?" the girl on the till asked.

"Manchester. All day." She gave the assistant a conspiratorial grin. "My husband's letting me loose with the cheque book in all those shops."

"Lucky you," the girl said enviously. "My old man goes hairless if I buy anything for myself."

"You've not got him trained properly."

"Have a nice time," the girl called as Jennifer walked out, then watched her drive off. "Good looks and a rich husband. Why not me, God?"

Charlotte Quinn was standing by her kitchen window finishing her breakfast coffee, looking out over the yards behind the Stricklandgate shops. She saw Duggie Lydden drive in and park his car. He climbed out whistling then glanced up and waved.

"Lovely morning, but a bit nippy!" he shouted.

Charlotte Quinn smiled back and nodded automatically, then stared into what was left in her cup as he disappeared into his own shop. She realised that the fleeting, meaningless incident had finally precipitated something. She felt self-disgust at even acknowledging Lydden's existence, let alone indicating some normality of behaviour towards him. The man she had just smiled at was cynically betraying the man she loved and she had reacted as though nothing was wrong. Conscience suddenly inflamed her self-reproach and bitterness; however difficult it would be, however much it hurt him, Charles had to know.

Late in the morning, Maltravers judiciously considered five variations of the same sentence he had put on the screen, selecting the best curtain line. In both his novels and plays, he worked on the well-tried principle that if he put enough effort into making sure the beginning and ending were right, his characters could somehow be relied upon to take care of the middle. He made his decision and four alternatives disappeared then he pushed the necessary buttons to save the final completed version, satisfied that more than a dozen rewrites of the last act had finally come right. Writing, as he so often had to explain to non-writers, consisted mainly of pounding out words in the hope that some percentage would actually be usable. If anyone asked him about 'inspirational writing', he questioned how their boss would react if they waited for inspiration before doing their job. From the living-room the telephone rang and then Lucinda answered it and spoke for a moment before calling across the hall to him.

"Gus! It's Tess. She's in a call box."

He went through and picked up the receiver. "Hi. How's it going?"

"Apart from darling Andrew not appearing on cue in the second act the other night, fine. I was on stage on my own for more than half a minute before they dragged the little prat out of the dressing-room. He bought me very expensive roses as an apology and I warned him if he does it to any of us again I'll stick them somewhere vital and very uncomfortable then sent him off to apologise to the others. Anyway, I've checked the trains and can get to a place called Oxenholme about half past four on Sunday afternoon. They say it's the nearest station."

"Yes, I know it," he told her. "I'll pick you up. Incidentally, I've just finished and you were right about what she'd do when she discovers the child was protecting the headmaster."

"Of course I was. Any woman would have behaved like that. Well done and I look forward to reading it when . . ." Her voice disappeared for several seconds beneath a stream of electronic pips. "Damn! I've got no more change. Love to Malcolm and Lucinda and I'll see you Sunday. Bye."

Maltravers rang off then went into the kitchen. "How about a walk? I haven't breathed fresh air for the past two days."

"Love to." Lucinda put down her pen. "It's only the weekly letter to Simon and I can finish it later. Let's go up the Treadle."

The Treadle was a hill rising more than five hundred feet out of the land about half a mile across the fields from Brook Cottage. A rough, narrow path wound through bracken and tough, twisted gorse trees before climbing to the summit topped with an old triangulation point and the remains of a wall, built for no discernable purpose. As they reached the exposed peak, the force of the gusting wind made them stagger.

"Enough fresh air for you?" Lucinda shouted above the blast.

"Too much of this could be fatal!" Maltravers gasped as they dropped down into the shelter of a small hollow. The view circled from distant Yorkshire dales, round to the outskirts of Kendal to the north then on to the coast twenty miles away, where thin sunlight picked up a gleam of water like a horizontal needle at the estuary by Grange-over-Sands. In front of them ran the road from Kendal to the motorway with the railway line from London to Scotland beyond it; as they sat on the grass a train clattered past. The houses of Attwater lay beyond the railway; although Brook Cottage and its neighbours shared the address, they were isolated more than a mile from the village itself.

"Is that Alan Morris's church?" Maltravers pointed to a dark grey spire on a low hill south of the village.

"Yes," Lucinda replied. "You can just see the roof of the vicarage next to it."

"How long's he been here?"

"Oh, ages — certainly more than twenty years."

"As long as that?" Maltravers sounded surprised. "I thought bishops shuffled the pieces round the diocese fairly regularly."

"Things don't change as often in places like this," Lucinda told him. "Alan's never wanted to move, not even after his wife died."

"Well if it's a living that pays for three hundred pound suits, I don't blame him," Maltravers said. "My brother-in-law's a residentiary cathedral canon, but Oxfam chic is the best he usually manages."

"St Mark's is worth peanuts," Lucinda corrected him, "but Mary — that was his wife — was the only daughter of a clothes manufacturer in Kendal and she and Alan had no children. Whatever the church pays him is pocket money."

Maltravers looked at the church again. "He gave me the impression of being unusually worldly the other evening. What does his congregation think of having a vicar storing up treasures on earth? Decent poverty and social conscience are expected these days."

"Not in Attwater," Lucinda replied. "They want a nice comfortable figurehead who tells them they'll all go to Heaven as long as they put something in the collection for the Bible Society and promises not to inflict the new communion service on them. They're very conservative."

"And what do you think?" Maltravers asked. "Is it a case of when in Rome . . . hardly the appropriate phrase, but you know what I mean."

"I don't mind," she said. "A few of us get impatient sometimes, but we don't make waves. Alan gives the majority of them what they want."

"Well, it's a broad church," said Maltravers. "It accommodates more secular types than Alan Morris."

They sat in silence for a few minutes, then Lucinda pointed at the road below them. "There's Duggie Lydden's car."

Maltravers strained his eyes as he peered down and saw three cars, at that distance no bigger than a child's toys, on the road far below.

"How can you tell at this range?" he demanded. "Or do you know more about cars than I do as well?"

"Gus, *everybody* knows more about cars than you do. Anyway, he's got the only Golf GTi with that metallic finish around here. I'm positive it's him."

They watched as the vehicles went on towards the motorway, Maltravers still unable to distinguish between them.

"Shouldn't he be at his shop?" he asked.

"Half-day closing in Kendal." Lucinda glanced at her watch. "Some shops stay open but a lot of the smaller ones still shut. Come on, it's turned one o'clock. Let's go back and have lunch."

As they made their way down the hill, Maltravers shaded his eyes against the sun, looking along the road away from the town, and realised he could just make out the roof of Carwelton Hall

53

before the land fell away into a dip. It did not look an impossible distance, but would have been an intolerable walk on the foul night he had arrived. He thought he could just make out one of the cars turning into the entrance but it was impossible to tell which.

In his vicarage, Alan Morris was wracked by nervous excitement and apprehension as he contemplated a final desperate means of escape from a nightmare more serious than he had ever thought possible. Attwater was a wealthy parish and there had been so much money available when his own had begun to dwindle. At first he had always been able to replace it and the various books had always balanced; then the juggling had begun with its crazy transfers from one account to another, running just ahead of the annual audits. But the amounts and the financial adjustments had grown until the whole edifice of deceit had begun to crumble and sway.

His protection had been years of visible, unquestioned honesty. He subtly drew attention to his probity — when he still exercised it — to maintain that reputation which made any suggestion of irregularity ridiculous. He was naturally trusted now because he had been trustworthy in the past. Only he knew that he had crossed into criminality so long ago that he was now indifferent about how far he went. His delusion was complete and essential to his defence and justification of himself; he could even persuade himself that this afternoon would solve everything.

Charles Carrington finished checking the conveyancing details of a house purchase he was handling then locked the documents away in his filing cabinet. He put on his overcoat and went into the secretary's office next to his own.

"I'm off, Sylvia," he announced. "If Sir Bernard calls again, say I'll get back to him in the morning."

"Yes, Mr Carrington. Oh, while you were on the phone, Mrs Quinn rang and asked if you could call her back. I told her you were leaving early this afternoon, but she said it was urgent."

The wall clock behind the secretary's desk showed ten past three. "I'm all right for a few minutes. Will you get her for me please?"

He returned to his office and stood by the window, waiting for the telephone to ring, looking out at the green dome of the Ashton Memorial in Williamson Park that dominated the town.

"Charlotte? It's Charles. What can I do for you?"

"Thank you for calling back." Her voice sounded partly relieved, partly agitated. "I have to see you, Charles. As soon as possible. It's very important."

"Well, I'm just about to leave for home but I'll be going straight out again once I've changed and won't be back until late," he told her. "Can it wait until tomorrow evening? You can come round and have a drink."

"No . . . no, not at the house. Somewhere private."

He paused for a moment. "The house is private Charlotte."

"I don't mean that, I mean . . ." She caught her breath. "I mean I want to see you alone."

Carrington sat down and leaned across his desk. "Charlotte, what are you talking about?" There was no reply. "Do you mean you want to see me without Jennifer?"

"Yes."

There was a silence while he waited for her to continue. "Charlotte, what are you trying to say to me?"

"You really don't know?"

"I'm not certain," he replied carefully. "But I want you to tell me. Now. On the phone."

She sighed very deeply. "Charles, you're not making this any easier for me. You really have no idea what I want to talk about?"

"Possibly, but I don't want to jump to the wrong conclusion."

"Stop being a bloody lawyer! You know full well and fine why I'm ringing! Don't you?"

There was a silence as Carrington sat very still, then he reached forward and began to rotate the ridged wheels of the perpetual calendar on the desk in front of him.

"I think you're trying to tell me that Jennifer is having an affair." His voice was very bleak and his sense of the inevitable was mingled with a perverse relief.

Charlotte Quinn's voice sobbed down the line for a few moments before returning very faintly. "When did you know?"

"Know?" Carrington said. "I only *know* now. But I've suspected it for . . . what? Two months? There is one other thing you can tell me though. Who's it with?"

She sniffed then almost whispered her answer. "Duggie Lydden."

The calendar showed Tuesday May 38, 1947. Carrington stared at the insane date for several seconds, then began to spin one wheel slowly again, the day, month and date staying the same, the years rising until the little window showed 1999.

"Charles? Are you still there?"

"Yes." The voice was now a lifeless monotone. "I thought it had to be him, but . . . well, it doesn't matter, but I think I'd have preferred it to be someone else."

"What are you going to do?"

"I was going home to change for a Masonic meeting in Carlisle," he replied. "But they'll have to manage without me. I think I'd like to talk to you. Can you come to Carwelton Hall?"

"What about Jennifer?"

"She's spending the day in Manchester and won't be back until this evening."

"What time do you want me to be there?"

"Four fifteen? I'll be back by then and . . ." Carrington hesitated. "And thank you, Charlotte, I appreciate how difficult this must have been for you."

"Oh, Christ, I should have told you before!"

"That doesn't matter. You've told me now and . . . I'll see you in about an hour."

He rang off before she had time to say anything more and she held the receiver to her ear, listening to the dialling tone. Suddenly she felt weak and sat down abruptly. She had finally done what for so long had terrified her and she began to cry with relief. Charles's first reaction had been that he wanted to talk to her; they had lost a lot of years, but there could still be more left when this was all sorted out and she had helped him through it.

In his office, Carrington reached forward and corrected the calendar, as though needing the ability to restore something to normality. He left without speaking to his secretary and within minutes he was on the motorway and driving away from the city.

As he made the half-hour journey to Attwater, cold numbness and disbelief that his suspicions had been proved gave way to a confusion of emotions. His lack of anger surprised him. He was unable to comprehend Lydden; to betray anyone so maliciously, particularly a friend who had helped you, was unimaginable behaviour. Towards Jennifer there was only a turmoil of feelings whirling through random memories. The first casual chat in his partner's office; the flowers he had bought for her birthday a few weeks later; hesitantly kissing her for the first time; the shared laughter over their deception in that hotel register in Lytham St Annes. Then later the ridiculous joy of their wedding, his delight at taking her to Carwelton Hall as his wife and introducing her to his friends. Had countless private, personal incidents meant so little — perhaps nothing — to her? The image of her opening the door to Lydden while he was safely absent at work, taking him upstairs, letting him fondle her and crying in ecstasy as their bodies locked together in bed was so appalling that he had to thrust it from his mind.

He left the motorway and drove through the villages to Carwelton Hall, stopping behind another vehicle in the drive. Glancing at it in surprise, he let himself in to what should have been an empty house. As he stepped through the door, there was a sound from the library across the hall and he walked towards it.

In Manchester, Jennifer Carrington was selecting a new tie for her husband, asking the assistant if she could recommend somewhere nearby for a cup of tea before going on to a dress shop she knew in Timperley on the south side of the city. Among her shopping was the Kingsley Amis book she had bought for him at Sherratt & Hughes.

Maltravers pulled the captain's chair up in front of the fire and took the photocopy of the last, completely unexpected, genuine Sherlock Holmes story out of the envelope. He turned to the first page and began to read just as Charles Carrington entered the library of Carwelton Hall, stopping in bewilderment as he recognised the figure standing by the wall safe. There was a thundering explosion and more than a hundred and fifty shotgun pellets ripped his chest and abdomen to pieces. The force hurled him into the air like a marionette then he crashed to the floor on his back. From a pattern of wounds across the lower half of his face, tiny streams of blood began to trickle and the life went out of uncomprehending eyes. As he died, Maltravers grunted with contentment as the mystery of *The Attwater Firewitch* began to absorb him.

AN ENCOUNTER AT BUSHELLS

Unlike many of his contemporaries, Sherlock Holmes was not a frequenter of the London clubs, whose sociable facilities held little attractions for his solitary nature. However one such club — Bushells, just off the Victoria Embankment — marked the start of one of his last cases.

We were taken there by Sir David Digby, Principal Under-Secretary at the Foreign Office, at the end of the day during which Holmes had resolved the Franco-Prussian crisis in the summer of 1890. His identification of watermarks on paper and knowledge of the chemical composition of inks had proved that the infamous Mannheim-Stern letters had been forged by a cell of anarchists working out of Hamburg and that the British Ambassador was innocent of any complicity with regard to the political assassinations which had shaken the Continent. Sir David's relief and gratitude outweighed his amazement at my friend's methods.

"Mr Holmes," he said warmly. "Your achievement is nothing less than having preserved the peace of Europe. While the details can never be made public, Her Majesty's Government owes you an immeasurable debt."

"Then I trust their gratitude will be reflected in their fee," Holmes remarked. "However, the matter is now resolved and, if you will excuse us, Watson and I wish to eat."

"As my guests," insisted Sir David. "Please accompany me to my club."

Holmes shrugged indifferently. He would have been as satisfied with a meal at the nearest artisans's eating house as dinner at an establishment renowned throughout London. As we walked the short distance from Whitehall, he was in a withdrawn mood I knew well. The demands of an investigation having been met, his mind had relapsed into a condition of inertia. We dined well on Dover sole — then, as now, a speciality of Bushells — before retiring to the lounge. Sir David greeted several members as we walked through and many glanced with interest at the tall, gaunt figure of his companion. We sat by a window affording an angled view of the Thames at a table already occupied by another man to whom Sir David nodded.

"Cedric Braithwaite," he explained, then turned to the other. "I need hardly introduce Mr Sherlock Holmes and Dr Watson, but I can tell you, Braithwaite, that I have today been privileged to observe this gentleman's powers at first hand and they are astounding indeed."

Braithwaite folded away his newspaper and regarded us with keen grey eyes. He was a well built man of about forty years of age with a strong face, somewhat weatherbeaten, and black wavy hair.

"I envy you, Sir David. Like so many, I am only familiar with Mr Holmes's exploits through the excellent accounts of Dr Watson."

I nodded in acknowledgement as he continued. "However, from reading those narratives Mr Holmes, it has occurred to me that the powers you utilise are not necessarily unique to yourself. We may all possess them, but lack the ability to use them."

Full of admiration for what Holmes had achieved that day, Sir David looked momentarily offended, but my friend spoke before he could utter any rebuke.

"You are quite right, sir," he replied. "I have said as much to Watson. However few, if any, exploit such gifts and are therefore surprised when another does."

"Then might I put my theory to the test?" Braithwaite

59

enquired. "I would be interested if you would make any observations about myself and then grant me the opportunity of trying to follow your reasoning."

Holmes smiled. "Very well, and I in turn will be interested in the results. You are a widower and a member of the legal profession living in the north of England. You own a house with extensive grounds, which you assist to cultivate yourself, and own a large dog. This morning you rose early to come to London and have been closely occupied with whatever affairs brought you here since your arrival. I could add more, but that will suffice."

"Correct in every particular, Mr Holmes," Braithwaite replied.

Sir David looked astounded and I, while very familiar with my friend's abilities, was unable to see how he had correctly deduced so much. Holmes, now relaxed after a splendid meal and an encounter with stimulating company, placed his slender fingertips together.

"Now, sir, you have your opportunity to demonstrate that you are not among the great mass of unobservant mankind."

"I would beg a moment for consideration," Braithwaite replied. "In you the gift is highly developed and you must allow for those in whom the skill is not so advanced."

He surveyed his own figure for a moment, then a look of realisation crossed his face.

"I can follow you in part." He held out his right hand. "I wear my late wife's wedding-ring. Were you sitting closer, you would observe it is scarcely worn. She died in childbirth less than a year after our wedding-day. That I am in this club indicates some probability that I am a lawyer but . . . ah, yes. From where you are sitting this document in my inside pocket with its distinctive red ribbon must be clearly visible. My accent betrays my northern origins, although surely I could possibly now live in London.

"The callouses on my hands, hardly the result of court work, reveal my horticultural activities and I now perceive some hairs on the edge of my coat, which my dog left when I walked him this morning. He is a red setter and they show up against the dark cloth. I did rise early and have been very busy, but there you have the advantage of me."

Holmes turned to me. "You see, Watson? All possess what gifts I have, few employ them — unlike this gentleman."

He returned his attention to Braithwaite. "I think you would eventually follow my other conclusions given time. The creased and dusty appearance of your clothes indicates a long train journey, presumably from your native north country; that you have not had time to have them attended to shows you have been actively occupied since your arrival. As in so many instances, it is your shoes that are of interest. A slight amount of clay is adhering to them. Of late, the weather throughout Britain has been dry but, even in London, I have observed a heavy dew in the mornings. This would dampen the clay and make it stick, but only in the early hours."

"Incredible!" Sir David exclaimed. "Although I am as impressed almost as much by your responses Braithwaite as by Mr Holmes's original."

"Prosaic," Holmes contradicted then looked at Braithwaite keenly. "But would you perhaps care to repeat the operation in reverse?"

Braithwaite laughed. "A most tempting offer! While we have been talking, certain points have occurred to me and I would welcome the opportunity. Very well. You also rose early and breakfasted in haste and some agitation. You spent the early hours in some location where the grass is long. For the rest of the time all your attentions were engaged upon an urgent matter. Dr Watson was with you in the morning, but I cannot speak for the afternoon. However, the doctor is now having second thoughts about his recent decision to change his hatter."

"Capital!" Holmes rubbed his hands together in delight. "You are a man after my own heart, sir. Now let me see . . . yes, there is an egg stain on my lapel. Mrs Hudson had cooked breakfast and it seemed churlish to refuse to eat. My haste is self-evident. As for the rest . . ." He looked down. "Ah, we are back with the morning dew which has left grass stains on the bottoms of my trousers. I spent the earliest part of the day in . . . I cannot be precise about the location, but a certain embassy in London has lackadaisical service in its grounds. My hands still carry ink stains picked up during the afternoon and the fact that I have not had time to remove them indicates the matter was pressing. We came straight here after the completion of the matter.

"Watson's trousers betray the same grass stains, however he was only present as an observer in the afternoon and there are no signs of what he was doing. I had intended remarking upon his unsatisfactory new hatter myself. The indentation around his forehead is still visible, even though he removed his bowler some time ago. Correct, I think?"

"Naturally," Braithwaite replied with a bow. "I am honoured to have had the opportunity of matching my poor wits against yours. My legal work as a Crown Prosecutor means it is possible our professional paths could cross. If that were to occur, the challenge would be formidable."

"And I would need to be on my mettle, sir," Holmes exclaimed.

"A compliment indeed," said Braithwaite. "Now, if you will forgive me, I must retire. I have to make an early start for my journey back to Westmorland tomorrow."

With a courteous nod to us all, he stood up and left the room.

"Sir David, that gentleman's company is the most entertaining I have enjoyed for some time," Holmes said heartily to our host. "I am grateful to you for introducing us. What do you know of him?"

"Not a great deal," the Under-Secretary replied. "He operates on the northern circuit and stays at Bushells when in London, which is where we met. He lives in Meldred Hall near Kendal."

"I partly know the town," said Holmes. "I was engaged there once on an investigation which Watson found too pedestrian to include in his chronicles. A good deal of my work is of that nature, despite the impression given by his selection of the sensational or bizarre which he says have more appeal to his readers."

Holmes smiled at me slyly. "However, Sir David, the hour is late and it has been a long day. I must return to Baker Street."

"The Cabinet will be made aware of what you have done at the first opportunity," Sir David promised. "It is regrettable that there can never be any public acknowledgement."

"I leave such honours to politicians," Holmes replied. "Mine is a more self-effacing business."

THE FIREWITCH LEGEND

Towards the end of the following March I called at Baker Street to find Holmes completing a late breakfast. Virtually all his post had been tossed to the floor, indicating it was from the sort of time-wasting eccentrics who frequently discommoded him, but one letter was engaging his attention.

"Good-morning, Watson. Do you recall our meeting with Cedric Braithwaite at Bushells last year?"

"Very clearly. Do I infer you have heard from him?"

"Yes, and a very curious letter it is. See for yourself."

As I took the note, Holmes went to the bookcase and, while I read, consulted a number of volumes. The address 'Meldred Hall, Attwater, Near Kendal' was printed at the top of the letter which was dated the previous day.

"Dear Mr Holmes," I read. "This is being dispatched before I catch this morning's train for London where I shall stay the night at Bushells. I pray you will be available to see me tomorrow morning so that I may place before you a matter of the utmost seriousness. It seems that my life may be in the gravest danger and I now fear also for my sister. The most incredible aspect is that there appears to be a connection with the family legend of the Attwater Firewitch. I regret approaching you with such scant courtesy on the basis of our

63

brief meeting with Sir David Digby, but beg you to believe that I am desperate to know where to turn. Cedric W Braithwaite."

I finished reading and looked up at Holmes. "What do you make of it?" I asked.

Holmes did not reply as he continued examining one of his books. He turned the page and read on, then closed the volume sharply and replaced it on the shelf.

"We know the measure of this man, Watson," he said. "He is clearly capable of handling most matters for himself. He would not consult me upon a trifle and his evident agitation amplifies the seriousness of the matter. I am also intrigued by this family legend."

"I have always believed you regarded legends as merely the products of fanciful minds," I remarked.

"They are," he replied. "But there is invariably some grain of truth behind the web of tales spun around it. However, none of my books refers to such a legend and I am puzzled by the term Firewitch."

"Surely it indicates the manner of her death?" I suggested.

"I think not. While witchcraft was regarded as a heresy in Scotland and on the Continent, bringing death by burning, in England it was a felony and those found guilty of it were hanged."

"Perhaps she dealt in fire in some manner?"

"Possibly, but the front doorbell indicates that our anxious visitor has arrived and will be able to furnish us with the answers himself."

Moments later Braithwaite entered. There was little resemblance to the man I remembered. He was highly nervous and confused, but the most shocking thing was several deep scratches, partly healed, down both sides of his face.

"Mr Holmes, thank God you are here!" he cried, then staggered forwards as Holmes leapt to his side to prevent him from falling.

"This way." He led our visitor to a chair. "Watson, the brandy."

I poured the drink which Braithwaite accepted with trembling hands. As he gulped it down, I was appalled that the confident and capable man I had last seen should have been reduced to such a pitiful condition. Holmes took a seat opposite him and waited until he had recovered some manner of composure.

"I had anticipated this was a serious business," he finally said quietly. "But I clearly have underestimated its gravity. Please tell me everything that has occurred when you are able."

"Thank you," said Braithwaite and finished the brandy at a swallow. "I hardly know where to start. Since leaving Meldred Hall, I have been haunted by the fear there will be some further outrage in my absence."

"Pray compose yourself," Holmes told him. "As recent events have evidently caused you great distress, might I suggest you begin with this legend to which you refer? That is clearly in the past and you may find it easier to talk about first."

"Yes, of course." Our visitor appeared to make an effort to regain his natural demeanour. "The legend of the Attwater Firewitch is little known outside our neighbourhood of Westmorland. It began in the time of my ancestor Thomas Braithwaite, who built the original Meldred Hall in the sixteenth century. There was a woman in the district named Margaret Seymour who had the reputation of being a witch. In our rational and scientific age, it appears preposterous that people could believe in such things, but then they had great potency. You may be familiar with Mr Harrison Ainsworth's excellent account of the Lancashire witches, events that took place just across the county border not far from my home around the same period."

"I have heard of the book, but its nature is not such as to engage my interest," Holmes commented. "Please continue."

"In the autumn of 1548, Margaret Seymour called at Meldred Hall begging for food," Braithwaite went on. "She was turned away somewhat curtly and was later seen gathering herbs from a hedgerow near the house. Shortly afterwards,

Thomas's daughter fell ill of an ague and the Seymour woman began to boast that she had placed a spell on her. I should add that she had a familiar in the shape of a strange bird, a matter of which you will shortly see the significance.

"As a Justice of the Peace, Thomas had her brought before him. She at first denied her claims but, when faced with witnesses who had heard her words, defiantly admitted them. She was sent for trial at Lancaster Assizes accused of witchcraft. The contemporary reports indicate that her incarceration had unhinged her mind and she rambled like a madwoman in the dock. She was found guilty and sentenced to hang.

"In the meantime, all efforts to alleviate the daughter's condition had failed and, the night before Seymour's execution, Thomas visited her cell to beg her lift the supposed spell. He was accompanied by a priest who wrote an account of the occasion."

Braithwaite produced a piece of paper from his pocket.

"This has been copied from the original, although some of the more antique phraseology has been modernised."

Holmes glanced through it then passed it to me, asking Braithwaite to wait until I had read it for myself.

"At the request of Thomas Braithwaite, Gent," I read, "I did accompany him to the Lancaster prison, to see the witchwoman Margaret Seymour, under sentence of execution, that he might persuade her to lift the Devilish enchantment placed upon his daughter, Jane, at that time lying unto extremity of death.

"The woman lay on a heap of straw in one corner and we could clearly see Satan's mark upon her, a gross protuberance upon her chin with several hairs springing therefrom. She was silent as Thomas Braithwaite beseeched her, for pity's sake, to spare his innocent child and I enjoined her to reject the Devil and all his works at peril of her immortal soul but to no avail. Then did Thomas Braithwaite fall into a great rage, crying that he would pursue her through all of Hell in his vengeance. I called down for the Mercy of God at such

66

blasphemy and pulled him away and as I did so she spat at him. But it was not spittle that landed on his cheek, it was the woman's blood.

"As I dragged him from the room, the woman spoke, making strange passes with her hands, which struck fear into my heart. She said:

> 'The bird will fly, the bird will land,
> The fire will come at its command,
> The flames will burn with scorching breath,
> The fire will ever bring you death.'

"Then did Thomas Braithwaite's rage increase greatly. He broke away from me and cried at the woman that he would bring fire upon her and it was with the greatest trouble that I did lead him from the cell."

I handed the curious narrative back to Braithwaite.

"The story thereafter is briefly told," he continued. "The morning after the visit, Margaret Seymour was taken out to be hanged, but as she was being led to the scaffold Thomas and a party of his servants rode up and abducted her. They took her back to his estate and locked her in a barn which they then set ablaze. As her cries faded, a great bird was seen to rise out of the conflagration. That night it reappeared on the roof of Meldred Hall and the daughter began to scream that she was burning. She died within minutes and the bird flew away. The curse of the Attwater Firewitch had come to pass."

As our visitor completed his strange narrative, Holmes leaned forward in his chair and looked at him piercingly.

"A melodramatic tale," he remarked. "But one which a man of your abundant intelligence would treat as nothing more than a historical curiosity exaggerated by added romantic imaginations. It is more than this which has brought you to me."

Braithwaite looked at him desperately. "Much, much more Mr Holmes. I have known that legend since childhood and it has never caused me concern. But now . . ."

He shuddered and his eyes went wild again. Holmes glanced an instruction at me and I went to pour another brandy. As I did so, Mrs Hudson entered and said that a porter from Bushells was at the door with an urgent message for our visitor. Holmes told her to bring him in. He was obviously a retired military man, well suited to the club's blue and grey uniform for its servants.

"Beg pardon, sir," he said. "But Mr Simpson, the club secretary, took receipt of this telegram and felt that it should be delivered to Mr Braithwaite without delay. He had mentioned he was coming here, sir."

"Thank you, my man." Holmes took the telegram and gave the messenger sixpence. As he saluted and walked out, Holmes handed it to Braithwaite who tore it open then leapt to his feet with a cry.

"My God! Eleanor!"

Before either of us could move, he had dashed from the room and we heard his footsteps pounding down the stairs and the crash of the front door. We leapt to the window and saw him frantically hailing a cab and jumping into it.

"We must follow him at once!" I cried.

"There is no urgency," said Holmes calmly. "There are no trains back to Westmorland until this afternoon."

"Is he returning there then?"

"Of course. A telegram of such importance could only have come from his home and its contents have clearly destroyed what capacity for logical thought he currently retains."

He turned from the window then crossed the room and picked something up from the floor.

"His telegram," he remarked. "His dropping it underlines the agitated condition of his mind." He read the message and his face darkened.

"This is no fanciful legend, Watson," he said grimly.

I took the telegram from his outstretched hand. It said:
'YOUR SISTER ATTACKED BY GREAT BIRD. RETURN AT ONCE.'

*

We were greeted at Bushells, where we had expected to find Braithwaite, with the news that he had already left to catch an earlier train to Manchester from where, we could only conclude, he would complete his journey on horseback.

"And a few hours' patience would have resulted in his being there at least as quickly," Holmes remarked. "When a rational man loses all touch with plain common sense, Watson, he is being driven hard. We will follow him this afternoon, using the train he has so impetuously abandoned. Are you at liberty to accompany me?"

"I have only to inform my wife and pack," I replied. "I have recently engaged a junior partner and the experience of dealing with the practice on his own will be a salutary one."

"At Euston station then." As I turned to go, Holmes called back to me. "Include your revolver in your luggage."

We purchased hampers of cold ham and chicken from the London and North Western Railway for our seven hour journey north and secured a compartment to ourselves. Holmes was disinclined to discuss the business towards which we were heading; theorising without data he left to dreamers. I tried to engage him in conversation about various reports in the late afternoon edition of the *Star*, but his interest was only aroused with an account of a double murder in Hammersmith. He listened attentively as I read the details concerning the discovery of the bodies of a man and a woman, both of whom had the letter x carved into their foreheads.

"The man was a minor clerk with a shipping agency and the woman the agent of a Mediterranean state with whom he had become entangled," he told me. "The arrival of a merchant ship from Naples a week ago sealed their fates and nothing could prevent it."

The conversation reminded me of something I had meant to raise with him previously.

"I have often wondered why you were not involved in the

infamous Whitechapel murders back in eighty-eight," I remarked. "They remain unsolved and I would have thought that the authorities would have called upon your services."

He gave me a curious look. "Of course they did, Watson, although by that time I had investigated the killings of my own volition."

For a few moments he remained silent, gazing through the window at the landscape as I waited for him to continue.

"I spent several nights in the area in a disguise so impenetrable my own brother Mycroft would not have recognised me," he said finally and there was a very sombre tone in his voice. Reflected in the glass of the carriage window, his face had become grave. "At the end I had proved that the conclusions I had reached following the murder of Martha Turner in George Yard Buildings were correct in every detail."

He turned to face me, and I was startled by his countenance. He looked like one recollecting the most terrible evil.

"You and I are in agreement, Watson, that certain stories like the Runnymede Cobra or the Casket of the Medicis must never be told. Better they were shouted from all the rooftops of London than that the identity of the Ripper and the full explanation behind his atrocities should ever be revealed."

I find it impossible to convey how much his reply shook me. The cases to which he referred involved persons and matters of the greatest consequence; exposure of the details of either would be calamitous. I found it incredible that a series of sordid murders of common women of the streets could be connected with matters of greater magnitude. But I can recall few occasions when my friend spoke with more gravitas.

Because of the severity of the gradients, the main line bypassed Kendal and we left the train at the small halt of Oxenholme some distance from the town. It was too late to go straight to Meldred Hall and we secured the services of a dogcart which took us to a travellers' hotel. Holmes asked the youth who showed us to our rooms if he knew the Braithwaite family.

"Yes, sir," he replied. "I help with the harvest on the estate each year. But 'tis terrible what has happened to Miss Eleanor."

"You have heard of that then?"

"All Kendal has. She was attacked by the bird of the Firewitch. Some say she is dead, but I think that be just rumour. I pray it is anyway."

Holmes thanked the youth and instructed him we would require an early breakfast the following day before dismissing him.

"This Firewitch still has her believers locally," he commented. "Any strange incident connected with Meldred Hall over the past three hundred years will doubtless have been attributed to her. An attack by a great bird, as the telegram says, would be natural fodder for folklore. Let us hope that the boy's prayers for Miss Braithwaite are answered."

The next morning we hired horses and took the direction indicated to us. Within little more than half an hour, we reached Meldred Hall, an imposing black Lakeland stone house behind a high wall on the road from Kendal to Sedbergh, hard by the village of Attwater. The house stood on the edge of a wide valley with the mountains rising about two miles to the west. The Hall had been built (I later discovered) some thirty years earlier in the Gothic revival style with mullioned arched windows and steep, gabled roof. Holmes presented his card to the butler and we were taken to the morning-room where Cedric Braithwaite joined us.

"Mr Holmes! Dr Watson! What miracle has brought you here?" His face even more drawn and haggard than the previous day.

"Nothing more miraculous than the steam engine." Holmes produced the telegram. "You left this in your haste. How is your sister?"

"Sleeping, thank God, but her experience has been terrible. I should never have left her. There is devilry in this place!"

"Then I am confident it will prove to be Man's rather than

Satan's," Holmes commented. "You left us yesterday with your story incomplete. Will you now tell us of more recent events?"

Braithwaite paused in his pacing by the fireplace and gazed at the flames leaping from the logs.

"The first real occurrence was on the sixteenth of January," he began. "I was walking through the woods about a mile from the Hall in the evening when a woman appeared about fifty yards ahead of me. She was bent and old and dressed in rags. She raised her stick and waved it at me in a gesture of threat. Then she hobbled away. I ran to the spot but there was no sign of her, despite the fact that she was too aged to have made away with any speed.

"I dismissed the matter from my mind, but about a month later I was again on the outskirts of the same woods in the evening with Prince my dog when he suddenly ran ahead of me. He stopped some distance off and began to paw at the ground and then . . ." Braithwaite turned from the fire and there was terror in his face. "And then, Mr Holmes, a huge bird, the like of no creature I had ever seen before, swept out of the trees. I heard Prince yelp in agony as it settled on him. I raced to the spot and began to strike at the creature with my stick. But it would not be driven off and one of its great wings knocked me to the ground.

"As I lay there, the creature plunged at Prince again then rose with something in its claws and flew back towards the trees. I scrambled to my feet and went to Prince. The poor animal had been torn to pieces. As I bent over his body, I heard a hideous laugh and looked up to see the same old woman at the edge of the woods holding a lighted brand above her head. I ran towards her, but once again she vanished."

"What description can you give me of this bird?" Holmes asked.

"Of immense size and of no colour I could discern in the gloom," Braithwaite replied. "But it bore two horns upon its head. I know of no such creature with such things."

"Two horns?" Holmes repeated thoughtfully. "An interesting detail. What happened next?"

"Up to the attack on Eleanor, the most horrible thing, which was what drove me to seek your aid. A week ago, again in the evening and near the woods, the same woman leapt out of a bush in front of me as I was returning to the Hall from my customary walk. She grasped hold of my coat and spat directly into my face then was gone. For a moment I stood stunned by the incident, then raised my hand to wipe my cheek. There was something red on my fingers and I realised it was blood. Then I heard a rush of wings and a great shape was upon me.

"It was the same bird, its talons tearing my face. I fought as best I could, but its strength was terrifying. In the struggle I fell to the ground, then the bird suddenly flew away again. I returned to the house and ordered a search of the area but nothing and nobody was discovered."

Holmes had become very grave as he listened to Braithwaite's story. "And your sister's ordeal while you were in London?"

"Almost identical to mine," Braithwaite said grimly. "She had visited one of our tenant farmers whose child is sick and was riding back across the estate when the same woman ran out of the trees and dragged her from her horse, then lashed her across the face. My sister is certain she screamed 'Beware the Firewitch!' before vanishing, then the hideous bird attacked. Mercifully, it flew off after only a few seconds as Eleanor fainted. When the horse returned without her, an alarm was raised and she was found, injured but alive, thank God. She was unconscious when they brought her back, but recovered sufficiently to tell her story before the doctor sedated her."

Braithwaite looked at us with an expression of despair. "What is the explanation for these atrocities and how long will it be before this bird brings death on its wings?"

"Compose yourself, sir," Holmes said sternly. "The terror of your experiences has affected your usual sense of judgement but I am not to be affrightened by the sudden recreation of ancient legend."

For a few moments, my friend stared at the ceiling in meditation.

"Your household staff," he said finally. "Has there been any recent addition to it?"

"The groom Johnson was hired last autumn, but apart from him the most recent appointment was the Scottish kitchenmaid McGregor who has been with us some three years. Four of my staff have been here since my father's day."

"And has anyone left your employment recently?" Holmes pursued.

"I dismissed Adams, the under butler, shortly after Christmas." Braithwaite indicated a decanter on the sideboard. "He had been stealing my whisky. He was not aware of the care with which Painter notes the level each evening. He denied it, but there were no other suspects and since his departure there has been no repetition of the thefts."

"And what have you discovered about him subsequently?" Holmes asked. "You would obviously have enquired."

"He sailed from Liverpool for America a month after he left here," Braithwaite replied. "He had secured a position as ship's steward."

"Then we must look elsewhere," Holmes said. "Can you accommodate Watson and myself at Meldred Hall?"

"Gladly," Braithwaite said feelingly. "I shall feel greatly comforted by your presence."

Holmes turned to me. "Return to Kendal and arrange for our things to be brought here, Watson. Now, Braithwaite, with your assistance I will commence my investigation into this curious and malevolent bird."

ELEANOR BRAITHWAITE'S NARRATIVE

I am obliged at this point to relate certain matters which took place during my absence. As I departed for Kendal, Holmes asked Braithwaite if his sister was sufficiently recovered that he might talk to her. Enquiries revealed that she had awoken and he was taken to her room.

Eleanor Braithwaite was twenty-three, dark haired and athletic with strong and beautiful features highlighted by deep brown eyes. However, when Holmes first saw her, there were several savage gashes upon her face, one of which had only just missed her right eye. He solicitously asked after her health and if she felt able to answer his questions.

"If they will help to solve this hideous business, I will make every effort, Mr Holmes," she replied weakly. "Although I do not know what I may be able to add to what my brother will already have told you."

"We shall see," Holmes told her gently. "Let us begin with the woman who pulled you from your horse. Did you see her face?"

"Only the merest glimpse just before she struck me," she replied. "It was filthy and of someone of about sixty years of age I should think. I did not recognise her."

"And with what did she strike you?"

"I'm not certain. A stick I fancy, but it felt sharp."

Holmes tenderly moved her head to one side. The principal wounds on her face ran downwards, but there were several other deep scratches running from her left ear towards the mouth.

"A bramble perhaps," he observed. "Very well. After the bird flew away, can you remember anything before you fainted?"

She shook her head. "I remember hearing my horse running and the hoot of an owl, but thereafter knew nothing until I woke up in this bed." She paused. "Oh, yes, of course! I heard the sound of laughter."

Holmes looked at her sharply. "Laughter has many voices. Can you be more specific?"

"Cruel laughter," she replied. "High pitched and vindictive."

"Like that of an old woman?" he asked.

"Exactly like an old woman."

75

Holmes rose and took her hand comfortingly. "Rest now. You are safe here and your brother will have all the protection I can give him."

He left the young woman with her maid and asked Braithwaite if he could interview the man who had led the search for her. This was the butler Painter, who had also dispatched the telegram. He was a grizzled man well struck in years, having been in the service of the family since before Braithwaite's childhood, but remained vigorous and alert.

"Henry the stable boy raised the alarm, sir, and we knew which route Miss Eleanor would have taken back from Lowman's Farm," he explained. "Past the mere, through Witch's Wood then across the meadows."

Holmes shot him a glance. "Witch's Wood?"

"Yes, sir. It is so named because Margaret Seymour the Firewitch, lived in a hovel there. It was she who . . ."

"I am familiar with the legend," Holmes interrupted. "I was not aware the woods had a connection with her. Complete the story of your search."

"We were approaching the wood when I heard Henry, who was some distance ahead, call my name," Painter continued. "He was kneeling over Miss Eleanor lying by the bridle-path. We carried her back and summoned the doctor. It was too late to send a telegram to Mr Braithwaite that night, but that was done first thing the following morning."

"You have mentioned the stable boy joining in the search," Holmes added. "Who else accompanied you?"

"Bates the gamekeeper, who was at the Hall that evening," the butler explained. "There were no other men available."

As the butler left, Holmes made several notes in his pocketbook, then turned to Braithwaite who had been present during the interview. "Your groom joined you comparatively recently. What do you know of him?"

"He was trained in the stables of Sir Henry Goodman near Coniston," Braithwaite replied. "Sir Henry recommended him after my previous groom died. He's a married man with a cottage on the estate and his work here has been of the highest order. Do you imagine. . . ?"

"My unalterable habit is deduction, not imagination," Holmes corrected somewhat tersely. "I would like to speak to him next."

They found the groom saddling the horse Braithwaite had hired at Lancaster on his journey from Manchester, in order to return it. He was a sallow faced, wiry individual, his spine bent like a shallow bow. Holmes asked why he had not been present to assist in the search for Eleanor Braithwaite.

"I was on my way home to my cottage," the man replied. "I knew nothing about it until I came back this morning."

"And who would have attended Miss Braithwaite's horse had she returned without mishap?" Holmes enquired.

"Henry, the stable lad. It would only have needed unsaddling and putting back in its stall after so short a ride."

"And where is your cottage on the estate?" Holmes added.

"About half a mile in that direction."

"Towards Witch's Wood?" Holmes remarked. "I see. Did you observe anything suspicious in that vicinity during your journey home?"

The groom shook his head. "It was dark, but I saw nobody about."

Holmes nodded and appeared satisfied, but as he and Braithwaite were leaving the stable yard, he turned back to Johnson.

"Upon which merchant vessel did you sustain the injury to your back?"

"The ss *Leonora*, sailing out of Whitehaven," Johnson was clearly surprised, but Holmes strode away before the groom could demand how he could have known the fact.

"I was unaware Johnson had been a seaman," Braithwaite remarked as they walked back towards the Hall.

"There was a nautical skill about the knots in that rope by the stable door," Holmes replied. "His short stature would have precluded enlistment in the Royal Navy, therefore his experience must have been as a merchantman. His present condition would have rendered him unsuitable for enrolment, so he was fully fit when he joined and suffered some mishap during his service.

"His maritime background may possibly be of relevance, but I was more interested in acquainting at least one member of your household with my methods. Johnson will tell the others, and if this mischief lies on your own doorstep, the culprit may make a false move out of apprehension. Now I wish to see the locations of these recent incidents."

Braithwaite took him first to the spot where his sister had been found. Holmes examined the ground, but the rescue party had obliterated anything that might have been of value. Straightening up, he looked towards a low belt of trees some distance away.

"Witch's Wood I presume," he commented.

"Yes. Beyond it is the mere on the shore of which is Lowman's Farm."

They went next to where Braithwaite had first seen the old woman in the woods. The area was overgrown with high dead bracken and bramble bushes. Working from the place at which Braithwaite said the woman had vanished, Holmes discovered a piece of cloth caught on a twig.

"Cheap cotton material woven on a mechanical loom, almost certainly in one of the Lancashire mills," he remarked. "Of possible consequence."

A search of half an hour yielded nothing more, then they emerged out of the trees and the mere spread before them. It was a shallow oval, four hundred yards at its widest point and rather more than half that in breadth. Gorse and heather grew round its circumference. Holmes followed its edge for some distance then produced his glass to examine several shoeprints in the soft ground.

"Dunlop soles, size seven," he murmured. "Made by a woman or a small man, possibly even a child, certainly running. They disappear as the ground becomes more firm and could have continued round the lake or gone off towards the hills." He made a sketch of the pattern. "A commonplace design, but it may be of value if we can locate the shoe that made it. I have limited experience of ghosts, but am not aware that they favour footwear manufactured in Northampton more than three centuries after their death. We are dealing with the living here, Braithwaite, although it may be as deadly as malignant spirits. Our last port of call will be Lowman's Farm."

Farmer Lowman himself was out completing the spring sowing, but his wife answered Holmes's questions. She had no recollection of any strangers in the area and was sure her menfolk would have commented if they had. After giving her attention to their sick daughter, Eleanor Braithwaite had left about seven o'clock and the time it would have taken her to reach the point of her attack tallied with the period it would have taken the horse to gallop back to Meldred Hall. Holmes finally asked Mrs Lowman if she had heard any reports of an unusually large bird seen flying in the locality.

"No, sir," the woman replied shaking her head. "We see occasional buzzards in the hills, but they rarely come down here into the valley."

They thanked her and returned to Meldred Hall, which is where I found them on my return and am able to continue my account as a first hand observer and participant.

Chapter Five

Frantic knocking erupted through Brook Cottage, hammering blows mixing with ceaseless electric chimes as somebody held down the front doorbell at the same time. Seconds earlier, absorbed in reading, Maltravers had not registered the screech of tyres scattering stones on the path outside and the slamming of a car door. Irritated by the interruption, he put down *The Attwater Firewitch* and went to answer it. Face distorted with horror, Charlotte Quinn stood in the porch.

"Thank God you're in!" she gasped. "I must use the phone!"

Before he could speak she pushed past him and ran into the cottage. When he followed her, she was in the centre of the living-room, looking around in agitation.

"Where is it?" she shouted. "The telephone!"

"On the piano . . . what the hell's the matter? What's happened?"

She leapt at the phone without replying, then stood with her hand on it, gulping with exertion and emotion.

"Who are you calling?"

"The police." She suddenly sobbed, the sound half caught in her throat. "They must get into Carwelton Hall!"

"Police?" Maltravers put his own hand on top of hers to prevent her lifting the receiver. "Hold it right there! Tell me first."

Charlotte Quinn's hand strained beneath his for a moment, then he felt it slacken. Her face was haggard as she turned to him.

"I rang Charles at his office this afternoon and told him about Jennifer and Duggie Lydden." Her voice shook again. "He said he wanted me to meet him at Carwelton Hall as soon as he got home. His car was in the drive, but there was no reply. Then I looked through the letterbox and saw him on the floor near the library door." She shuddered and began to weep. "Gus, I think he's dead!"

Maltravers stared at her. "Dead? How could you tell?"

"He was just lying there! I shouted but he didn't move. There was blood . . ." her voice croaked as she sobbed violently.

"Did you try to get in?"

"Of course I did!" Anger flared out of her frenzy. "I wouldn't be here otherwise would I? Stop asking stupid questions."

She thrust his hand aside and snatched up the phone, continuing as she began to punch the 9 button. "He must have killed himself because of what's been happening. He suspected it before I told him and . . . police! Quickly!"

She waited a few seconds then repeated part of what she had just told Maltravers. She hung up and stood very still with her shoulders bowed, then suddenly threw back her head and screamed. Maltravers put his arms round her and she trembled against him like a child in the arms of its mother woken from a nightmare.

"What did the police say?" he asked as she grew calmer.

"They want me to go back and meet them there." There were tears of desperation in her eyes as she looked at him pleadingly. "Come with me, Gus! I can't go . . . I can't . . . Oh, God!"

"Of course I'll come," he assured her. "We'll use my car, you're in no condition to drive."

Moments after Maltravers turned on to the main road at the bottom of the lane, they heard the hysterical soprano whoop of a siren before a police car appeared behind them over the rise from the direction of Kendal, headlights blazing and blue alarm light flashing on the roof. It swept past and Maltravers accelerated after it. As he skidded to a halt on the gravel drive of Carwelton Hall, two policemen were at the top of the front steps, one crouched at the letterbox. He straightened as Maltravers and Charlotte Quinn dashed up to them. Balloon fat and pencil thin, the policemen had an irresistible resemblance to Laurel and Hardy, an insane touch of comic farce.

"Mrs Quinn?" the fat one asked. Charlotte nodded. "I can see him. We'll never force this door though. Is there any other way in?"

"No. I tried the back but it's locked."

"It's a window then."

He ran down the steps and took a hand axe from the car boot. The front windows were set several feet off the ground and Laurel had to climb on Hardy's shoulders to smash the pane and reach for the catch before scrambling inside. Seconds later the front door opened. Maltravers held Charlotte Quinn's arm as they followed the second policeman into the house. She waited with him just inside the front door as the officers knelt by Charles Carrington on the far side of the hall. He was lying face upwards in the doorway of the library, head and shoulders on the floor.

"I'm afraid he's dead." The fat one laid down Carrington's wrist. "An ambulance is on its way. Can you come with me please?"

Still supporting Charlotte Quinn, rigid with shock, Maltravers followed him into the lounge. The other policeman had returned to the car.

"Is it all right if I give this lady a drink?" Maltravers asked. "I know where it's kept."

The officer nodded and Maltravers went to the cabinet. "Here you are," he said gently and she sipped obediently, then sat with the glass clenched between white-knuckled hands on the tweed skirt of her suit.

"Mrs Quinn's in no state to talk at the moment," Maltravers said. "I'll tell what little I can though."

"First of all, I'd like to know who you are, sir."

"My name's Augustus Maltravers and Mrs Quinn called you from the cottage of friends of mine where I'm staying. She said Mr Carrington had arranged to meet her here this afternoon but when she arrived she saw him through the letterbox. I came back with her."

"Does Mr Carrington have any family?"

"Only his wife as far as I know," Maltravers replied. "However, I saw him first thing this morning and he mentioned that she was spending the day shopping in Manchester. He didn't say when he expected her back."

"Thank you, sir. My colleague is calling the duty inspector who will inform the CID. They will want statements from you both. For the time being, I must ask you to remain in this room and one of us must stay with you."

"Of course." Maltravers sat next to Charlotte Quinn. She squeezed his hand absently as he took hold of hers, but did not look at him or speak. Maltravers saw an ambulance arrive outside and then two more cars pulled into the drive. There were voices in the hall before another man entered the lounge, tall and broad with a tough, penetrating face beneath a helmet of dove grey, almost white, hair.

"Good-afternoon," he said. "Detective Sergeant Donald Moore, Cumbria CID. I've been told what's happened and I'd like to speak to you first, madam. Will you please go with this officer, sir?"

Maltravers smiled encouragingly at Charlotte, then was taken to the dining-room across the hall. Instinctively he looked at the body again, blood hideously splashed across the chest. Carrington's arms were raised above his head and the two ambulancemen were like silent witnesses at a crucifixion. After about fifteen minutes Moore joined him and he repeated his brief story.

"We'll need full statements at the station, sir," the sergeant said when he had finished. "But there's one point you may be able to help us with now. Do you know what Mr Carrington kept in the library safe?"

"The safe?" Maltravers frowned. "He . . . just a minute! Are you saying that. . . ?"

"I'm not saying anything, sir," Moore interrupted. "Can you tell me anything about the safe and its contents?"

Maltravers paused, analysing the question. "You've just told me an awful lot. That safe contained some books, but not any old books. In fact I doubt if there's anything in this entire house more valuable." He looked at Moore enquiringly. "But they're not there now are they? And that means Charles Carrington was murdered."

"I can't comment on that, sir. Tell me about these books."

As Maltravers and Charlotte Quinn were taken to Kendal police station, Carwelton Hall was filling with urgent activity, the blinding glare of a photographer's flashlight, increasing numbers of police swarming through the house, methodically beginning their search, combing the floor of the library, dusting for fingerprints. A man with an open black bag beside him was kneeling by Carrington's body, holding dead lips around a clinical thermometer.

"Are you all right?" Maltravers asked quietly as the police car pulled away. Charlotte nodded.

"Just about." Her voice was toneless. "He's been murdered hasn't he?"

Maltravers could almost feel the policeman in the front passenger seat listening.

"I'm afraid it looks that way," he replied.

They remained silent for the short journey then were taken into separate interview rooms. Maltravers explained about the Conan Doyle books and how he knew that Carrington had kept them in the safe. From the questions he was asked, he pieced together a certain amount of information. No, he did not know if Charles Carrington had owned a shotgun; that took care of the weapon. Yes, he could remember who else had been in the library after the dinner party when Carrington had showed him a copy of the book although, apart from Malcolm Stapleton, they had been strangers. Douglas Lydden, who had a business in Kendal, the Reverend Morris and a man called Geoffrey Howard. However he was certain that other people knew of the existence of the books. They had been in Carrington's family for a hundred years and there was no suggestion he made any secret about owning them.

"When Mr Carrington opened the safe, did he mention what the combination was?"

"The combination?" Maltravers's mind raced as the question triggered suggestions. "No, he just opened it."

"Could you see what the combination was from where you were standing?"

"No, it was on the other side of the room."

"And was anyone next to Mr Carrington at the time? Or perhaps nearer than you were?"

Maltravers frowned as he tried to remember exactly where everybody had been standing, then he shook his head.

"Morris was next to me and Malcolm and Howard were discussing some pictures on the wall near the fireplace. Lydden was looking at a book on the other side of the room." He paused. "You want to know if one of them could have seen the numbers, don't you? That's impossible. They'd have needed better eyesight than a hawk. I think I was the only one watching him, and all I could make out was that it was a combination lock."

But of course, he told himself, you're also telling me that the safe had not been forced, so somebody knew how to operate it — or made Carrington do it for them. But that meant . . .

"Just a minute!" He stared at Moore in bewilderment. "You're saying the safe had been opened by somebody aren't you? I'm sorry, sergeant, but that's impossible."

"I'm afraid it's been done, so it can't have been."

"Well it is," Maltravers replied bluntly. "Unless you can explain this. Charles Carrington told me he was the only person who knew the combination for that safe and there was no reason why he should lie about that. And the safe has a duress signal fitted — you must know how they work."

"Naturally." Moore replied cautiously. "What do you know about them?"

"It's an alarm system where if someone forces you to open your safe, you add one number to the combination. The safe opens all right, but the moment you put in the extra number, a bell rings at a central control. There's no sound in the house of course. The centre immediately calls the police and can tell them exactly where someone is in trouble. It's very sophisticated. Did you receive such a call?"

"I'd have to check, but I'm not aware of it," Moore acknowledged.

"Then you see what it means. If someone had experimented with the dial hoping to stumble across the right combination — and they'd only have one chance in a hundred million of success — the alarm would also go off. On the other hand, Charles would have put in the special number if he was being made to open it. Either way, the balloon goes up."

"Perhaps he didn't add the number."

"Oh, come on," Maltravers said disparagingly. "There's no point in having a system like that if you don't use it."

Moore looked thoughtful for a moment. "Would you excuse me, please?"

He left the interview room and Maltravers began to try and think of answers. The alarm would operate down a telephone line and could be cut off by severing the wire — but the police would discover that. Was the system simply out of order? Possible, but that could also be checked. Then would Carrington have told him he was the only one who knew the combination when there was someone else? Maltravers could see no reason to believe that. He was still wrestling with it when Moore returned.

"We received no alarm call," he admitted. "We'll examine the safe, but unless the system's faulty or was cut off, I have to agree with you. So how was it done?"

"Don't ask me. But I'll be fascinated to learn the answer."

An hour later he signed his statement and was told he could leave; his car had been brought from Carwelton Hall to the police station. Charlotte Quinn was waiting for him in the foyer.

"They told me you wouldn't be long," she said. "Will you come back to the flat with me? I don't want to be alone at the moment."

"Why don't you come with me to Brook Cottage?" he suggested. "I must tell Malcolm and Lucinda what's happened and they'll want to see you. Anyway your car's still there."

"Of course it is. I'd forgotten."

She sounded weary, as though the simple practicalities of collecting her car were too much to deal with. Maltravers took her arm as they walked to the police station car-park and could feel her trembling. As they drove out of Kendal across the River Kent towards Attwater, she sat with her head bowed, unconsciously folding and opening a handkerchief on her lap. When Maltravers reached across and pressed her hand comfortingly, she looked away and said nothing. Lucinda and Malcolm appeared out of the cottage as they arrived.

"We've heard." Even in the darkness, Maltravers could see she had been weeping. "The reporter doing police calls at the *Chronicle* picked it up and Malcolm rang me at school. I tried to call both of you, but there was no reply and we guessed you must know something about it when we found Charlotte's car here."

She walked over to Charlotte Quinn and hugged her. "I'm so very, very sorry." She held her arm around the other woman's shoulders as she led her into Brook Cottage and through to a chair in the living-room.

While they listened to Maltravers relate the events of the afternoon, Lucinda made constant quiet gestures towards Charlotte, touching her gently from time to time, consoling with sympathetic, concerned smiles. As he lit a cigarette, Maltravers noticed that his hands were shaking.

"That's all we know. But there are a few things I've worked out from questions they asked me. Charles was killed with a shotgun and there is an unanswerable problem about how the safe was opened." He explained about the duress signal and the combination. "And something else has occurred to me. If the murderer meant to force Charles to open the safe, not knowing about the alarm, how did they know he was due home early instead of whatever time he usually arrives in the evening?"

"How did you know?" asked Malcolm.

"Because Charles mentioned it this morning when he dropped off the Sherlock Holmes manuscript. That's when he said Jennifer was spending the day in Manchester."

"And did she?" It was the first time Charlotte Quinn had spoken since they entered the cottage. The rest of them looked uncomfortable.

"What do you mean, Charlotte?" Lucinda asked cautiously.

"She would have known Charles was coming back in the afternoon," she replied. "She could have been there."

"That's a big conclusion to jump to," Maltravers said quietly.

"Isn't it just?"

An echoing silence followed the remark, then Lucinda stood up.

"I'm going to start supper. Can you give me a hand, dear?"

Charlotte held Maltravers's gaze defiantly as Malcolm went with his wife into the kitchen.

"And would it really make it any better if it was her?" he asked.

She looked away into the fire for a long time. Searing hatred was smothering the grief etched in her face as she turned away from the flames.

"In some ways it would. Except that they won't hang the bitch."

Her eyes went back to the fire to prevent him seeing anything more that was in them. Since calling Charles Carrington, she had been dragged through a swirling rack of emotions; apprehension at finally telling him, relief and rushing renewed hope at his wanting to see her, horror and anguish at the sight of his body. While she had been waiting for Maltravers at the police station, she was aware that something had happened to her. She could not yet identify the sensation now appearing in the dark, convulsive pit of her feelings, but when her numbness and paralysis began to fade she would know it and face it and obey it.

Jennifer Carrington started as she saw the police car outside Carwelton Hall. She stopped behind it and a policewoman got out and walked up to her car as she wound down the window anxiously.

"Mrs Carrington? I'm sorry, but I'm afraid there's been an accident."

"An accident?" She opened the door, leaving the engine running. "What's happened?"

"One of my colleagues inside will tell you."

Confused thoughts tumbled through her mind as she followed the policewoman to the front door, which had been opened while they had been talking. A man was standing in the light; like the police, he should not have been there.

"Dr Bryant?" She shook her head in confusion. "What's happened?"

"Come in please, Jennifer." Bryant led her into the lounge then sat beside her on the settee. Two other men were in the room and she stared at all of them in confusion. "These gentlemen are from the police and have asked me to be here because I have some bad news. I'm dreadfully sorry, but Charles is dead . . . all right, I've got her!"

Jennifer Carrington slumped into his arms with a moan as the policewoman leapt forward.

"Bring my bag," Bryant said as he supported her. "On the table."

The policewoman held Jennifer Carrington while he filled a hypodermic from a small phial of colourless liquid.

"This won't knock her out, but it will calm her." He pumped the syringe to remove any air. "She'll be able to answer your questions. Give me her arm."

He pushed up the wide coat sleeve and was about to make the injection when Jennifer Carrington's eyelids fluttered and she straightened up.

"It's all right, I . . ." She pulled her arm away. The pretence of fainting had given her time to think, but she did not want any sort of drug in her. She needed to keep her mind clear while she discovered exactly what had gone wrong.

"I'm sorry. Just a moment." She breathed very deeply. "That's better. I don't need anything. Just . . . just tell me what's happened."

"Mr Carrington was found dead this afternoon, madam. It appears he was murdered. We were told you were spending the day in Manchester and had no means of contacting you. We're sorry to have to question you at a time like this, but this is a very urgent matter."

"Yes," she said hesitantly. "Yes, of course. But who found him?"

"A Mrs Quinn. She called us immediately."

"Charlotte?" New, urgent questions raced through Jennifer Carrington's brain. "But what was she doing here? What time was this?"

"Mrs Quinn called us shortly after four-fifteen. She had come here to meet your husband."

Why? Jennifer Carrington was about to ask more then decided too many questions might be dangerous. She would have to be very careful.

"I'll try to help you," she said. "But can I have a drink please?"

By the time Bryant had poured it for her, she had prepared herself. She answered calmly as one officer asked questions while the other took notes. She had last seen her husband shortly before half past seven when he had left for the office and she had set off for Manchester herself half an hour later. Everything had been

89

normal. He had been due back in the afternoon to change for a Masonic lodge meeting in Carlisle. His secretary would know what time he left the office and it would have taken him about half an hour to reach Attwater. Then the police asked about the safe in the library.

"The safe?" She looked puzzled. "What's the matter with it?"

"The safe was empty when we found your husband's body, Mrs Carrington. We believe the murderer must have stolen the contents."

They were approaching the moment Jennifer Carrington had rehearsed over and over again, but now the script had been altered. She took another sip from her glass, trying to decide how to play the new scenario. She had to make some comment about the safe.

"Charles kept some very valuable books in there," she said.

"Who knew about them?"

"All sorts of people." Jennifer Carrington shrugged and looked helpless. "You knew didn't you, Dr Bryant? About the Sherlock Holmes books? Lots of our friends did. Charles's partner and . . . there must be others. I can't tell you them all."

"We'll need to know everyone you can remember Mrs Carrington. Nothing else appears to have been taken, although we'll need your assistance to confirm that. Perhaps if you could come . . ."

The CID man stopped as Jennifer Carrington suddenly cried out; she had decided it was too risky trying to change her story at the last minute. This had to come out now as planned.

"*No!*" Bryant, who was still sitting next to her, jumped as she screamed, dropping her glass and leaping to her feet. He stood up and took hold of her arm, but she shook him off violently. "No, he can't have! I never thought he . . . oh, God!"

The policemen looked at each other sharply as she started to cry hysterically. A pool of whisky from the lead crystal tumbler at her feet seeped into the carpet. Bryant and the policewoman made her sit down again. The CID officers waited silently.

"Who can't have what, Mrs Carrington?" one of them asked finally.

There was no reply as she sat with her head lowered; she appeared numbed, but she found that her mind was now working with surprising clarity. Bryant put his hand under her chin and raised it.

"Jennifer, you must tell them everything you can," he said. "You know something don't you? What is it?"

Her face was guilty as she turned to the police again.

"I've been having an affair," she said tonelessly. "With . . . with a man called Duggie Lydden. And he once talked about stealing those books."

"When was this?"

"I'm not sure . . . a few weeks ago, perhaps more."

"Do you know if this person owns a shotgun?"

"A shotgun? Do you mean. . . ?" She looked appalled. "I'm not sure, but . . . yes I think he does."

"And how did Mr Lydden plan to steal the books?"

She bowed her head again and began to turn the engagement-ring on her finger abstractedly. Then she reached down and picked up the fallen glass, putting it on the occasional table beside her.

"I'm not sure he actually planned it, he just talked about it. He owes my husband money and I know he was having difficulty keeping up the repayments. He'd said things were getting very serious and . . ." She hesitated. "I'm sorry, perhaps I'm wrong. I told him at the time not to be so stupid. But when you said you wanted me to tell you everybody who knew about the books, I suddenly remembered . . . I could be dreadfully wrong . . . I thought he was just joking. He must have been."

"We'll have to talk to him. Can you give us his address? And in the circumstances I must ask you to accompany us to the police station so that . . . no, I'm sorry doctor, Mrs Carrington seems able to give us a statement. You may come as well if you wish."

Bryant took her in his car, one of the CID men sitting in the back. She had worked out the dangers of the new situation, but could do nothing about it. She had to blame Duggie Lydden. After she had repeated it in her statement, despite Bryant's protests, the police said she would have to remain in custody until they made further enquiries. As a policewoman stood by the door, Jennifer Carrington sat in an interview room, sipping a cup of tea impassively. One thing had gone wrong, but with everything else that had been done it could still work.

"Mr Douglas Lydden? My name is Detective Sergeant Donald Moore from Cumbria CID and these are two of my colleagues. We are investigating a serious offence earlier this evening and wish to talk to you about it."

Lydden scowled as he looked at the large and forbidding plainclothes men on his front step, shadowy and menacing against the silver-blue neon light of the lamppost opposite. It was nearly half past eleven and he had just returned from a pub. Out of habit, he had made a pass at the barmaid and had been angrily warned off by her boyfriend who he had not realised was standing at the other end of the bar. It had been a humiliating end to a bad day.

"Serious offence?" His voice slurred. "What's it got to do with me?"

"We would prefer to discuss that inside if you don't mind, sir." Moore's impassive, patient official courtesy was very calm, but carried tangible irresistibility.

"And if I do mind? Do you know what bloody time it is?"

"We're fully aware of that, sir. I must advise you that we have a warrant to search these premises."

"A warrant?" Lydden looked alarmed. "I want my solicitor here."

"Perhaps we can come in while you call him."

For a moment, Lydden appeared ready to argue then stalked back into the house without a word, leaving the door open. When the police entered the front room, he was at the telephone. He swore as he misdialled, then tried again.

"Jack? Duggie Lydden. I've got the bloody police here and they say they've got a search warrant. Get over here . . . I don't give a shit if you're in bed, I want you here now!"

The solicitor arrived after quarter of an hour and asked to see the warrant then advised Lydden to co-operate. Before the search began, Moore asked a question.

"Do you own a shotgun, sir?"

Lydden looked defensive. "What if I do?"

"We'd like to see it, please."

Lydden glanced at his solicitor who nodded, then he went into the hall and opened the door of a cupboard under the stairs. He stepped inside and almost immediately came out again.

"It's not there." He seemed surprised. "Someone must have stolen it."

"Under the conditions of your firearms certificate, you are required to keep a shotgun in a secure place," Moore commented. There was no lock on the cupboard door. "Has there been a break-in at this house to your knowledge? No? Very well. When did you last see the weapon?"

Lydden shook his head, clearing muddled thoughts. "About a week ago I think. It's usually there with the cartridges."

"So you keep both gun and ammunition together in an insecure place?" Moore challenged mildly. "That is another offence."

"Sergeant, aren't you being a little heavy-handed?" the solicitor objected. "Three of you arriving at this time of night for a minor breach of firearms regulations? Really."

"It's not a minor breach, but that's not why we're here," Moore corrected. "We are now going to search this house."

At one o'clock in the morning, Moore told Lydden he was under arrest and cautioned him. In the loft the police had found a case containing the Sherlock Holmes books and the letters about them which Charles Carrington had also kept in the safe. After Lydden had given a statement about his movements during the day, the police questioned Jennifer Carrington again. Then both of them were held in custody.

Chapter Six

Spread on the invisible grapevine of a close community, news of the death of Charles Carrington raced electrically through Kendal and its surrounding villages the next morning. At Brook Cottage the telephone constantly rang with people excitedly asking Lucinda if she had heard, then almost invariably adding comments of their own. One said it was well known that Charles Carrington had received threats on his life, although she had not the slightest idea who had made them or for what reason. Another insisted — with a distinct air of satisfaction — that Jennifer had already been charged. Three different men were confidently named as the killer; one was even said to have made a full confession. Conflicting explanations involved various combinations of murderers and death by gunshot, knife or strangulation. Maltravers found a certain black humour in it all.

The first definite information came when Malcolm rang with details from a police press conference.

"They've confirmed everything we know," he told Maltravers. "And someone is helping with enquiries. You know the usual line."

"Are they saying who it is?"

"No, but you can't keep something like that quiet in Kendal. The word is that it's Duggie Lydden. Pick the bones out of that."

"Duggie Lydden? Christ." Maltravers felt disgust. He had hardly known Charles Carrington, but was appalled that someone could have murdered him. That the killer might turn out to be his wife's lover he found particularly repulsive, a civilised man's violent death besmirched by an additional sordidness. "And what about Jennifer?"

"Mrs Carrington is also continuing to assist the Cumbria CID with their investigation. And I quote. She's in police custody."

"Were they in it together then?"

"They've pulled them both in quickly enough. No charges yet though."

Maltravers thought for a moment. "Does Charlotte know all this?"

"I imagine so. Just about everybody else seems to," said Malcolm. "Hell, she was bitter enough when she left us last night. She'll go berserk if it turns out that Jennifer really was in it with him. I'll keep you posted if I hear anything else."

Lucinda looked questioningly as Maltravers rang off, then dismay spread across her face as he told her.

"Duggie Lydden! God, I knew he was a bastard, but . . ." She shook her head as if trying to dispel something revolting. "And Jennifer as well!"

"We don't know anything for certain," Maltravers pointed out. "The police haven't charged either of them yet . . . but murder is a curiously domestic crime. Most victims are close relatives of their killers."

"God, it's sick!" Lucinda said bitterly. Maltravers watched her walk into the kitchen and start to clear the breakfast things. Suddenly she raised a plate above her head, smashing it down on to the edge of the sink with a cry, then stared at the broken pieces at her feet.

"Just leave me alone, Gus." Without looking at him, she held her hand out warningly as he moved towards her from the living-room. "I'll be all right. I just don't like hating people this much."

Unshaven and haggard from a pounding hangover and lack of sleep, Duggie Lydden looked resentfully at Detective Chief Superintendent Brian Lambert across the plastic top of a table in the interview room at Kendal police station. The officer in charge of the murder enquiry was a Falstaffian figure, fingers like sausages and a concertina of jowls rippling below his chin. But his voluminous, clumsy physique swathed in a brown suit containing enough material for a modest tent, smothered the fact that his mind could move as fast as the whippets he bred. Disproportionately small eyes, sharp as shreds of coal, flashed swiftly through two sheets of paper with Lydden's signature at the bottom. Wary and attentive, Lydden's solicitor sat at one end of the table across which the other two men faced each other. Lambert put the papers down.

"Just to go over your statement again, Mr Lydden." His voice was like a great engine rumbling in the hollows of a tunnel. "You went to Carwelton Hall shortly after one o'clock yesterday afternoon where Mrs Carrington was waiting for you. You went to bed with her then left about an hour later, after which you returned to your shop in Stricklandgate and spent the rest of the afternoon stocktaking. Is that correct?"

"Yes."

"Do you wish to add to that statement or amend it in any way?"

"No."

Lambert's wooden chair creaked alarmingly, legs bowing outwards as he leaned back, dropping the statement on the table and rubbing a thumb fat as an egg against the side of his nose.

"Mrs Carrington has informed us that she left Carwelton Hall early yesterday morning, spent the entire day shopping in Manchester and did not return until the evening, by which time the police were at the house," he said blandly. The solicitor glanced sharply at his client. "Do you have any explanation as to why she should tell us that?"

"She's lying."

"One of you certainly is," Lambert commented impassively. "Have you yet remembered any witnesses to your movements during the afternoon, particularly between about three forty-five and a quarter past four?"

Lydden shook his head. "No. But somebody could have seen my car in the yard behind the shop."

"Enquiries are continuing, but so far we've found nobody who can vouch for your statement," Lambert told him. "However, I should advise you that Mrs Carrington has been able to produce certain evidence to corroborate her story and, from what we have been able to ascertain at this stage, it appears to be correct."

Lydden made no response, but his solicitor shuffled uncomfortably in his seat.

"And do you now have any explanation for . . ." Lambert's body eased forward with the menace of a toppling rock and he picked up the papers again, consulting them briefly and unnecessarily, ". . . the discovery in your house of ten volumes of a book by Sir Arthur Conan Doyle and other documents, known to have been the property of Mr Charles Carrington?" Deceptively bland, pinprick eyes questioned beneath elevated eyebrows.

"I've told you already. I don't know how they got there."

"And you still have no idea where your shotgun is?"

"The last time I saw it, it was in the cupboard. It must have been stolen."

Lambert regarded him in silence for a long time before Lydden's eyes dropped to the table again.

"Mr Lydden, you could save everybody a great deal of time if . . ." Lambert began with exaggerated patience. Lydden exploded into anger.

"I've got nothing more to say! I've told you the bloody truth and she's lying! Now either fucking well charge me or let me out of here!"

The superintendent paused, then leaned heavily on the table top and heaved himself up, collecting the papers as he did so. More than six feet four inches tall, it was as awe-inspiring as seeing a whale slowly raising its mass out of the sea.

"Your solicitor will confirm that the police have a right to hold a suspect for questioning, initially for up to twenty-four hours, Mr Lydden," he said. "If necessary we can request a further period of police detention. Our enquiries are continuing. I think it will be best if you discuss your situation further with your lawyer."

The bleak room seemed suddenly empty as he walked out and went to the office set up for his use, where Moore was waiting with a fax report.

"From Manchester police, sir," he said. "Further support for Mrs Carrington's account of her movements yesterday."

Lambert took the document and the great wall of his face creased into a humourless smile as he read it.

"If it goes on at this rate, we may have to let that lady go soon," he remarked. "She looks well in the clear. What have forensic got?"

"Lydden's are the only fingerprints on the suitcase," Moore replied. "And there are only his handprints on the loft. It's the standard square of wood in the ceiling of the landing that you have to push up."

"What about on the books?" Lambert asked.

"Most have no prints at all," Moore said. "But Mrs Carrington says they were hardly ever taken out of the safe. We've only found the victim's on two of them. Carrington's are also the only prints on the safe door, but there's evidence of Lydden's presence in various parts of the house, including the library. Doesn't prove anything of course. He was there the other evening for dinner and Mrs Carrington is making no secret of the fact he was her boyfriend. We knew that from Mrs Quinn's statement before she admitted it herself."

Lambert's whole face trembled like a jelly as he shook his head.

"And still nothing to back up Lydden's story about being in his shop all afternoon? No? Well perhaps he'll change it for us, particularly if we can find that shotgun. Any luck so far?"

"No, sir. We're still searching his house, but it could be anywhere."

"And what about this question of how the safe was opened?"

"We've had the manufacturers check the alarm system and it's working normally," Moore replied. "We've questioned Mrs Carrington, but it seems certain she didn't know the combination. Carrington's partner has been able to confirm that. But somebody opened it, because there's no way it was forced."

Lambert's tiny eyes almost disappeared as the lids squeezed about them. "We've got to sort that somehow. Lydden's hot favourite at the moment, but a defence lawyer could drive a bloody coach and horses through a hole like that. See what you come up with."

As Moore left, Lambert lowered his bulk into a chair then read through all the evidence again. The forensic report said Carrington had died instantly and more than a hundred and thirty pellets had been extracted from his body during the post mortem; others had been picked out of the frame of the library door and the wall of the hall. In her statement, Jennifer Carrington insisted she had refused to have anything to do with Lydden's suggestion to steal the books and had forgotten all about it, convinced he had not been serious.

Thoughtfully plucking at the thick ripples of flesh below his chin, Lambert considered it all. Finding the shotgun could be a critical factor in forcing Lydden to abandon his version of events with its so far unsupported alibi. That was a straightforward matter of searching. But the safe combination. . . ? Lambert didn't like that. He was not greatly concerned about Lydden sticking to his story at this stage; he had known villains persist in swearing black was white all the way to the judge sending them down for life. But the apparently impossible could plant reasonable doubts in the mind of a jury. It would solve a lot of problems if Lydden simply made a full confession and explained the currently inexplicable. The police's initial natural suspicion that Jennifer Carrington could have been involved was fading as evidence to prove she had been in Manchester all day was becoming very persuasive.

Lucinda was teaching again that afternoon and Maltravers was alone in Brook Cottage when Charlotte Quinn rang.

"Have you heard?" she asked. "About Duggie and her?"

"A certain amount," he replied cautiously. "Although we're still waiting to see if Malcolm finds out anything more through the paper."

"Well, it's obvious, isn't it?" she said. "She must be behind it all. And he's such an idiot that he let her go to Manchester for the day so she'd be in the clear."

"I'm not sure I follow you."

"Can't you see? She must have told him he could share her alibi, that she'd tell the police he was with her. Now she's double-crossed him. She'll pretend she knew nothing about it and Duggie won't be able to prove she did. She'll have made sure of all the witnesses she needs to prove she was miles away. Christ, she's been clever."

"But if that had been their plan, the police would have asked all sorts of questions and the possibility they could have been giving each other an alibi would have been obvious," Maltravers argued.

"Jennifer's intelligent enough to realise that, but she could have persuaded Duggie it would work. You don't know how stupid that man is."

"Then what about that safe? Do you think Charles would have told me he was the only person who knew the combination if it wasn't true?"

"No," she agreed reluctantly. "But the police will find out how he did it eventually. I just pray they can prove she was in it as well."

"You want that a lot, don't you?"

"You don't know how much. Do you blame me?"

Charlotte Quinn slammed the phone down, angrily biting her lips to stop herself crying again. She had shed too many tears for too long for Charles and where had it got her? Now, as something began to crawl out of the pit inside her and identify itself, she heard its increasing, insistent voice temptingly whispering the only absolution.

At six o'clock that evening Maltravers and Lucinda arrived at Kendal police station and asked the desk sergeant if they could talk to someone investigating the murder. They had finally remembered seeing Duggie Lydden's car while they were on the Treadle the previous lunchtime.

"I'm sorry we haven't come forward sooner," Maltravers apologised to the detective constable in the interview room. "With everything else, it went out of our minds. But we understand you are holding a Mr Douglas Lydden in connection with the death of Charles Carrington."

The officer looked at him sharply. "How do you know that, sir?"

"My husband is editor of the *Cumbrian Chronicle*," Lucinda explained. "He was told by one of their contacts. Anyway, everybody in Kendal knows."

"Very well." The acknowledgement was guarded. "Mr Lydden is assisting us with our enquiries. What information do you have?"

When Lucinda had explained, he questioned her closely about the time and if she was certain it had been Lydden's car.

"Absolutely," she insisted. "Well, put it this way, nobody else I know of in this area has one like it. It could have been a stranger passing through, but it would have been a great coincidence."

"And you saw the vehicle too, sir?" the officer asked Maltravers.

"I saw a car which Mrs Stapleton identified for me," he corrected. "However, I can only distinguish between a Rolls-Royce and a Reliant by counting the wheels, and even then I have to remember which of them only has three. But Mrs Stapleton was quite certain."

"Then I don't think we need bother with a statement from you, sir." The policeman sounded condescending, as though ignorance about car identification indicated some unfortunate mental shortcoming. "Mrs Stapleton can include in hers the fact that you were together."

They left with a warning that the police might wish to call them as witnesses at some future court hearing, but when Lucinda's statement was taken to Lambert he was dismissive. It only confirmed Lydden had been in the neighbourhood of Carwelton Hall at lunchtime on the day of the murder; as he did not deny that— although he still insisted Jennifer Carrington had been there as well — eyewitnesses were academic, unless they had seen him leave and return to his shop and remain there.

"I expected a better reaction to what you told them," Maltravers remarked as he turned up the lane to the cottage. "What you saw could be important. Unless of course they've got a confession out of Lydden."

"Do you really think he could have done it?" she asked.

"I just find it . . . I'm not sure." Maltravers looked dubious. "I knocked down Charlotte's theory about him and Jennifer being in it together and I'm still positive she's wrong. But there are still things that don't make sense, apart from the safe business. For instance, why would Lydden. . . ?"

"Good God!" Lucinda jumped as they reached Brook Cottage and the reflection of Maltravers's headlights glittered off a scarlet Fiesta parked by the green. "That's Jennifer's! What's she doing here?"

"We're about to find out," said Maltravers. "But the widow Carrington doesn't appear to be helping with police enquiries any more."

Chapter Seven

"Charlotte found his body at four fifteen!"

The sentence had been waiting to leap out of Jennifer Carrington as her fingers nervously twisted the coiled ivory flex of the telephone in Carwelton Hall, waiting for an answer. After her release on police bail, she had extracted more information from her solicitor as he drove her home.

"What!" The man's voice shouted down the line at her. "What was she doing there?"

"God knows. She might even have seen you."

"No, there was nobody about, but . . . you know what it means?"

"Of course I do! I've been thinking about nothing else. The police have only just let me go."

"What about Lydden?"

"They're still holding him, but he hasn't been charged yet. My solicitor told me he'd heard the police found the books all right. But what if he manages to come up with an alibi?"

"He can't have done so far . . . calm down." He could hear her sobbing. "It's working. When can you have the books back?"

"Not yet, but if they charge him they apparently might be prepared to let them go."

"Well they should find the gun eventually, which ought to be enough for them. Once you get the books you can bring out the safe thing. We just carry on the way we planned."

"Come here," she pleaded.

"Not at the moment, but I'll be there soon."

"But I can't stand it on my own!"

"Then go and see somebody." He sounded impatient. "Act

naturally. People will expect you to want to talk about it. Tell them about Lydden. The more people who think he's guilty the better. Call me tomorrow."

He rang off abruptly because he wanted to think, not listen to Jennifer's anxiety. Had Charlotte Quinn seen him? No, because she would have certainly told the police if she had. But her inexplicable arrival could prove disastrous. If the police would just charge Lydden and release those books . . . then he could decide what to do.

As Lucinda and Maltravers entered the room, Jennifer Carrington was sitting on a high-backed wooden chair by the fire, an untouched drink on the table beside her. Face pinched and without make-up, brazen hair hastily and carelessly brushed, arms clasped protectively in front of her, she looked like a frightened child.

"Hello." Her voice was thin and brittle. "I'm sorry, but I had to come somewhere and you were the only people I could think of. I hope you don't mind. Malcolm said it was all right."

"When did the police release you?" Maltravers asked.

"A couple of hours ago. I went back to Carwelton Hall because I had nowhere else to go. I've got friends in Manchester, but I couldn't face driving there after what's happened. It was all right at first, but then I turned the Ansaphone on." She started to cry.

"Some people have been jumping to conclusions," Malcolm explained. "Jennifer's told me that one even said that she now had everything she wanted. They didn't leave their name."

The girl raised her head pleadingly to Lucinda, face wet with tears. "They were all so cruel! I had to get out. You didn't know Charles before I met him and I thought . . ." She took hold of the arms of the chair as if to stand up. "I shouldn't have come. Perhaps you . . ."

"No, it's all right," Lucinda interrupted firmly. "We're not going to throw you out. You can tell us what's happened if you want to."

Lucinda's face was expressionless as she sat down next to Malcolm. Maltravers remembered the incident in the kitchen when she had smashed the plate after hearing that the police were holding Jennifer and Lydden. Her feelings then would not be instantly shaken off.

"Gus and I would like a drink as well, please," she said and Malcolm went to the cupboard in the wall.

"How are you feeling?" Maltravers asked.

"Fairly bloody." Jennifer Carrington gave a sickly smile. "You know the police wouldn't let me go at first, don't you? They were all right about it and my solicitor was there, but they kept asking questions and I became confused. Then they released me, although I must let them know where I am."

"But are they still holding Duggie Lydden?"

There was a sudden flash of anger. "God, I hope they are! After what he's done!"

"You think he killed Charles?"

"There's no other explanation." For a moment she stared into the fire before looking directly at Malcolm and Lucinda. "Can I get one thing straight? If it offends you, I'll go, but I want it out in the open right from the start. Duggie and I were having an affair."

She looked defiant, as if expecting some reaction of offence.

"Jennifer, we've known that for a long time," Malcolm told her.

"What?" She sighed. "And I thought we'd kept it secret."

She took a sip from her glass, then continued with controlled calm.

"I'm not going to apologise for what I did, even after what's happened. You know how much older Charles was and . . . well our physical relationship wasn't enough for me." She looked at Lucinda. "You'll understand. I was frustrated. I loved Charles but I needed . . . all right, I needed sex."

Lucinda nodded non-committally. Jennifer Carrington dropped her eyes. There was a touch of bravado as she continued.

"Anyway, I did it and I don't care what anyone thinks because it didn't mean anything. I knew there would be no emotional involvement with Duggie. I tried to be discreet, although if you knew perhaps I wasn't very good at it. That was all there was to it, but I never dreamed where it would lead to. Dear God, I didn't."

"Let me tell you what we know," Maltravers interrupted. "Charles called here early yesterday morning to drop off the Conan Doyle photocopy and said you were spending the day in Manchester. In the afternoon Charlotte went to meet him at Carwelton Hall and found his body. She came here to call the police and I went back with her."

"The police told me about Charlotte." Jennifer Carrington brushed a fleck of dust from her skirt. "Do you know why she was meeting Charles?"

"He wanted her to for some reason," Maltravers replied evasively. "I didn't ask her why at the time and it didn't seem to matter later."

He knew he could rely on Malcolm and Lucinda not to add anything as he continued. Jennifer Carrington was listening to him very closely.

"Anyway, we were there when the police broke in and had to give statements. We gathered from what they asked us that the books had been stolen. Later we heard you and Duggie were in custody. That's about it."

Jennifer Carrington pushed back a stray strand of hair and sipped her drink again. She had not realised how involved Maltravers had been and was becoming aware that he was taking in everything she said; catching the flutter of leaping flames from the firelight, his very blue eyes never left her.

"Malcolm was telling me why you've just been to the police," she said. "You saw Duggie driving towards Carwelton Hall."

"Lucinda saw what seemed to be his car on the main road from Kendal," Maltravers admitted. "But we can't be certain where he was going."

"Oh, he's not denying being at the Hall." She paused, as if sorting out what to say. "Let me tell you what's happened. When I got home, the police told me about Charles and that the books had gone. I can't remember everything, but I blurted out that Duggie must have done it."

The blue eyes narrowed. "Why did you say that?"

"Because he'd suggested it to me. He actually said I should take the books and go off with him and we could make a fortune."

"That's ridiculous," Malcolm objected. "As soon as he tried to publish those books he'd have been arrested."

"Of course he would." Maltravers lit a cigarette. "But there are other possibilities. There are rich collectors who are not particular about how they obtain priceless items for their private pleasure. There would be no shortage of unscrupulous buyers for the *Mona Lisa* if it ever fell off the back of a lorry. On the other hand . . ."

He stopped, although he had not meant to continue. He wanted to let Jennifer Carrington guess at what he was thinking and see if anything came out. If she had been mixed up in the murder with Lydden, but had double-crossed him — as Charlotte had suggested — then the books could eventually become hers and there would be nothing to stop her publishing them. Certainly not conscience. There was also the matter of the safe combination; he wanted to find out how much she knew about that.

"Anyway, what did you tell him?" he added.

"Not to be stupid." She looked at them appealingly. "He was changing the rules. I would never have done something like that to Charles! Oh, I *know* what you're thinking. If I could sleep with another man then why should I have any feelings for my husband? Everyone gets so moralistic about it. But it wasn't like that."

"Preaching morals is a risky business for most people," Maltravers commented. "Anyway, that's irrelevant. The point is that when you heard the books were gone, you suspected Lydden. Have you any idea what happened when the police talked to him?"

"Oh, yes and I don't know whether to laugh or be sick," she replied resentfully. "When they came back to check his story with me, he'd said he had been to Carwelton Hall at lunchtime, met me there and we'd made love before he left at about two o'clock."

"But you were in Manchester all day." Maltravers stretched forward and flicked ash into the fire. "Weren't you?"

Jennifer Carrington looked at him sharply as he sat down again. His face was blank and it was impossible to tell if there were any suspicions behind the casual question.

"That's what the police wanted to know and at first all I could think of was that I'd stopped for petrol at the garage in the village near the M6," she replied. "But even I realised that only proved I'd set off. Then they asked about what I'd done in Manchester and I showed them receipts for the things I'd bought. I mentioned I'd drawn some money from a cash dispenser at a bank on Deansgate and they wanted to see the receipt for that as well. Did you realise they have the time on as well as the date?"

"I'd never noticed." Lucinda sounded surprised.

"Well they do, and it showed ten twenty-nine," Jennifer Carrington continued. "I went straight from there to Sherratt & Hughes to buy a book for Charles and paid with my credit card, so the shop must have the copy of the Visa form I signed. After that I had coffee in St Ann's Square and wandered round Debenhams on Market Street for a while before lunch.

"In the afternoon, I did some more shopping in the city centre — I bought Charles a tie among other things — then drove to a shop in Timperley and spent quite a while there looking at dresses. After that I went to a friend's house and I know it was six o'clock when I got there because she said something about arriving just in time for a drink. They gave me a meal and I left about half past eight."

"And people will remember you in the shops?" The inflections of Maltravers's voice made the question ambivalent.

"I'm not sure about the bookshop or Debenhams because they were both busy. But they'd certainly remember in Timperley because they know me there and I chose a dress they're altering for me."

"Well the cash dispenser and credit card receipt seem to take care of the morning," Maltravers acknowledged. "And Lydden is still saying he met you at Carwelton Hall at lunchtime? Why?"

"God knows," she replied. "I *told* him I was going to Manchester yesterday. The only thing I can think is that he's trying to drag me into it with him. He can be very vindictive. He might be assuming I'd not be able to prove where I was."

"How did he get into Carwelton Hall?" Malcolm put in.

Jennifer Carrington looked remorseful. "I gave him a key after he let me have one to his place. That was when it was all a bit silly. I'd forgotten all about it. I've lost the one he gave me."

She rubbed her hand down the front of her leg as though she was cold. "But there's another thing. My solicitor learned that the police found Charles's books hidden in Duggie's house."

"And have you any idea how he's explained that little difficulty?" Maltravers asked. "Is he suggesting you put them there?"

"Not as far as I know," she replied evenly. "But if he can tell the police what he's told them about me meeting him at Carwelton Hall, he could come up with any crazy explanation . . . except for one thing. I can't see how he opened the safe, because Charles was the only person who knew the combination and it . . ."

"And it had a duress signal built in." She glanced at Maltravers in surprise as he completed the sentence. "Charles told me about that after dinner the other evening and I pointed it out to the police."

"So that's why they asked me about it. They wanted to know if I knew the combination."

"And do you?"

His persistent questioning was beginning to make her nervous. Instead of simply accepting that she did not know, he turned it back on to her.

"No, and I didn't want to. If I have a couple of drinks I chatter on about anything and I knew how important those books were to Charles. I'd have felt dreadful if something had happened because of me. It came up when Stephen Campbell visited us once and his wife asked about it. Charles explained about the alarm and told her my feelings. He said nobody but himself knew the combination now, but it was in a sealed envelope with his will in a strongbox at the office which was only to be opened on his death."

"What did he mean by saying nobody knew it now?" Maltravers asked.

"It had always been known in the family, but Margaret — his first wife — and the children were dead. There was nobody else."

"Certainly not Duggie Lydden," Maltravers remarked. "So how was the safe opened? Campbell could have had access to the strongbox."

"Stephen?" Jennifer Carrington sounded incredulous. "Even if he had he would never have looked in it. I used to be his secretary. He's absolutely honest."

Maltravers threw his cigarette end in the fire. "There's something else I don't understand. How could Duggie have known Charles was due home early yesterday afternoon, if his idea was to force him to open the safe? Who told him?"

"I certainly didn't."

"I'm not suggesting you did. But who else knew?"

Jennifer Carrington paused for a moment. How many more could she suggest? "His secretary of course, and other people in the office. He might have mentioned it to someone at the Masonic lodge he was visiting. There could be others."

"Including me, because I saw Charles in the morning," Maltravers remarked drily. "And I've got a lousy alibi. Sitting alone in this house reading, with no witnesses until Charlotte arrived after the murder. But it wasn't me . . . and would Charles have told Duggie Lydden?"

"He might have done." Jennifer Carrington spoke as if something had just occurred to her. "I don't think he was going to the meeting, but Duggie's a Mason as well."

"And if he did, Duggie would have known you were in Manchester because you told him, and the house would be empty when Charles came back," Maltravers commented thoughtfully. "Yes, that's possible."

He suddenly decided to say nothing more. Finishing his drink, he went to pour more for all of them. As he put water in Malcolm's whisky in the kitchen, he was forced to accept that, whether Lydden had acted alone or Jennifer had been in it as well and was now double-crossing him, everything foundered on the question of how the safe had been opened. Her story about Campbell and his wife being present when Carrington had said he was the only one who knew the combination could be checked easily enough. And it was unimaginable that Carrington would have told Lydden. Maltravers stared at his reflection in the darkened, uncurtained window over the sink in front of him. The vision of the open safe was like some incredible conjuring trick; the impossible performed before your eyes. If he could only see the secret compartment, the hidden mirror, the ingenious machinery in the box . . . but this was not magic, it was human cunning. As he returned to the living-room, Lucinda was insisting that Jennifer should stay.

"You're not going back to Carwelton Hall at the moment," she said firmly. "And we're certainly not letting you spend a night alone in a hotel. You can think again in the morning."

She overrode feeble protests, but Maltravers felt Lucinda's offer was tinged with reserve. They kept up some sort of conversation throughout a meal which Jennifer Carrington picked at, then she went to bed in the second spare room with night things Lucinda lent her. Maltravers and Malcolm were finishing the washing-up when she came down again.

"And what do you make of all that?" Maltravers waved around a glass he had just dried, looking for somewhere to put it.

"Just leave it on the table," Lucinda told him. "Well, I'd never do to my husband what she did to Charles, but I expect some women would. I'll keep my opinion to myself."

"It doesn't matter if she'd been screwing her way through the Kendal telephone directory in alphabetical order," Maltravers told her. "But was she involved in murdering Charles?"

"Do you think she was?"

"Everything she's told us about Lydden is ridiculous," he replied. "He's got motive and opportunity coming out of his ears, but instead of coming up with even a half-decent alibi, he claims he met Jennifer at Carwelton Hall after she'd apparently told him she was going to be more than seventy miles away in Manchester, and it seems she can prove it. On a scale of stupidity from one to ten, he's scoring eleven."

He replaced the towel on its wooden rail fixed to the kitchen door.

"But look at her story for a minute. She draws the money from the cash dispenser about half past ten and goes to Sherratt & Hughes. The shop's only a few minutes' walk from Deansgate, so the whole process would take about quarter of an hour at most. She then drives back to Carwelton Hall, arriving around noon. After meeting Lydden like he says, he goes off, she gets back in the car and can be in Timperley on the other side of Manchester by the time she says. It's possible, although . . ."

Lucinda gave him a pitying look as she interrupted. "Oh, brilliant, Gus. I know dozens of women who'd break off in the middle of a day's shopping to make a hundred and fifty mile round trip for a quickie. I've got very mixed feelings about Jennifer at the moment, but I can't see her doing that. And even if that happened, what does it prove? Duggie could still have gone back to the Hall later."

"Back to the drawing board, I think," Maltravers agreed. "But why hasn't he simply denied being anywhere near Carwelton Hall yesterday and produced some story to back that up?"

"We may not have been the only people who saw his car," Lucinda pointed out. "Perhaps somebody else did and he knows it, which is why he's not risking saying he never went there at all. And remember what Jennifer said about thinking he was trying to drag her into it as well. Duggie Lydden can disguise it when it suits him, but if we use your same scale of stupidity for nastiness, he'd score twelve."

"She's right," Malcolm added. "Duggie's made a lot of enemies, and not just by fooling around with other men's wives. He can be a very unpleasant little bastard. But we're still left with that combination. How could either Jennifer or Duggie have known it? Or anyone else for that matter?"

Maltravers shook his head. "That, Watson, is clearly a three pack problem."

"Three pipe surely, Holmes," corrected Malcolm.

"Not in my case, I smoke cigarettes. Which reminds me. There's a book upstairs I must finish."

Maltravers looked at the photocopy of *The Attwater Firewitch* for a long time before opening it. It was eerie. A private book about the greatest of fictional detectives and an imaginary mystery had become a focal point of a real murder in the same house a century later. He reflected grimly that if Charles Carrington had been less conscientious about a family obligation to Conan Doyle and allowed the book to be published, he might not have died. And Maltravers had misgivings about Jennifer being able to produce a seemingly watertight alibi for the whole day; people's lives were not usually so conveniently organised by chance. She had cheated her husband who was intelligent; could she also have cheated her lover, who was apparently stupid?

He turned to where he had reached when Charlotte Quinn's

arrival had interrupted him and became engrossed again in harmless fiction.

THE MELDRED HALL STAFF

After luncheon, I joined Holmes as he interviewed the remainder of the household, beginning with Mrs Broom, the plump and excitable cook.

"'Tis the Firewitch!" she interrupted immediately Holmes began. "Margaret Seymour has come back again!"

"Again?" Holmes queried mildly. "Have there been previous visits by this apparition, then?"

"Of course there have, sir. Anyone born and bred round here knows about her wicked ghost."

"Most fascinating," Holmes said, giving me a secret wink. "However, I wish to know about your involvement the evening Miss Eleanor was attacked."

"I was just giving Bates the gamekeeper a bite to eat," she replied. "He'd called on his way home to see Alice McGregor — I think there'll be news from that quarter soon — but she'd begged me to let her go to Kendal to visit a friend of hers. There was little to do, Mr Braithwaite being away, so I let her leave when she'd finished the washing-up.

"Bates and me were chatting in the kitchen when we heard a horse gallop into the stable yard. We thought it strange Miss Eleanor should ride it so hard, but before we had time to see what was amiss, the stable lad ran in, saying it had returned alone. Mr Painter and Bates went off with the lad.

"I was in such a state while I waited! They carried her in to the kitchen and I cleaned those wounds on her poor face with my own hands. The doctor said I'd done well."

Mrs Broom folded her arms, indicating her story was complete.

"At what time had you last seen Johnson the groom that day?" Holmes asked. The cook's brow furrowed thoughtfully.

"He came in for his midday meal which he always has at the Hall. Then I saw him in the afternoon when I went out into the yard for a breath of air. I can't recall after that."

Before dismissing her, Holmes asked if Bates was expected at the Hall again that evening. Mrs Broom confirmed it was his regular practice to call after completing his duties. Holmes then asked her to send in the two kitchen maids. Both were greatly distressed, with Alice McGregor still lamenting her absence when she might have assisted in attending to Miss Braithwaite and her colleague Janet Hemsdale, a local girl, almost hysterical.

"People say the bird breathes fire!" she insisted at one point. "Lord save us all from the Firewitch!"

"If you avoid the area around the woods, no harm will come to you," Holmes assured her.

"We are safe nowhere!" she protested. "There is a curse on the Hall!"

"This is the first I have been told of it. What has happened?"

"Ill luck." Hemsdale shuddered as she replied. "Alice cut her hand when she fell out walking the other week. Cook dropped a whole set of plates in the kitchen. And Simpkins broke one of Miss Eleanor's favourite pieces of china while she was dusting."

"A series of minor household mishaps do not amount to a curse," Holmes told the girl sternly. "Such nonsense can be of no assistance to anyone."

"Forgive her, Mr Holmes," said McGregor. "Janet's always been of an excitable nature."

"Then you and your colleagues must urge her to temper it. Your duty is to support your master and Miss Eleanor, not indulge in stupidities. That will be all."

Holmes sighed as the door closed. "One would expect some degree of apprehension in this house, but such childish superstition as that girl Hemsdale is showing is intolerable. It is clear that the womenfolk among the staff are unlikely to be of much assistance."

His comment was confirmed by the upstairs and downstairs maids. One solemnly warned him that the great bird could make itself invisible and would attack anyone who angered its mistress. As they left, he made a sound of amused frustration.

"A necessary exercise, but of little value," he said.

"Little progress then," I observed.

"My investigation thus far has not been without accomplishment," he corrected. "The footprints by the mere locate this mischief in this mortal world and there are certain points concerning these attacks."

He enumerated them on his fingers. "One, they all occurred in the vicinity of Witch's Wood. Two, they all took place in the hours of darkness or closely approaching them. Three, Braithwaite and his sister were each attacked by the woman before the bird appeared. Four, the bird withdrew after a relatively short time, causing the death of the dog, but leaving its human victims injured but still alive. There is a space of about a month between the first three attacks, then the fourth takes place within a few days. Pieces of the picture, Watson, imperfect at present, but emerging."

He looked reflective for a moment. "And we must not, of course, overlook the business of the under butler."

"Adams?" I asked in surprise. "Did he not join the ship at Liverpool?"

"We can have every confidence in Braithwaite's ability to ascertain so elementary a fact correctly. Adams is as innocent of these attacks as he was of stealing the whisky from the decanter."

"How can you be certain of that?" I demanded. "And if it was not him, who was the culprit?"

"As under butler being trained by Painter eventually to assume the senior position, we may safely conclude Adams had ready access to the cellar and its contents," Holmes replied. "If the man had a propensity for an illicit drink, he would not have needed to steal it from a decanter where his theft would become so evident.

"I do not know who did steal the whisky, but there is no evidence it was consumed by anyone in the household. The inferences from that are obvious and possibly of the first importance."

Holmes spent an hour in Braithwaite's library, then I accompanied him to the cottage where Johnson the groom lived. His wife confirmed he had returned about six o'clock on the evening of the attack on Miss Eleanor then had gone out after supper for his regular game of cribbage at the nearby public house in Attwater.

"Where are you and your husband from originally?" Holmes asked.

"Johnson was born and bred in Whitehaven. After his accident, he joined Sir Henry's stables, which is where we met. I worked as a scullery maid at Coniston Manor, having been brought up in the village.

"Mind you," she added, "my husband's grandmother on his father's side was a Kendal woman and he still has kin in the town. We always go and see them on his monthly day off."

With apparent casualness, Holmes extracted further details regarding Johnson's connections with the locality, including the address of his cousin, then we rose to leave. By the front door, I remarked on a fine brass telescope in its case on a table.

"A souvenir of your husband's former career," I commented.

"Yes, sir," said Mrs Johnson. "He misses the sea and often walks out to the mountains across the valley from where he can watch the ships through it. He says that . . ."

Mrs Johnson was interrupted by a violent knocking on the cottage door. Henry the stable lad was standing outside, clearly in some agitation.

"Mr Holmes, sir!" he panted. "The master asked me to find you. Can you come back to the Hall at once?"

"What has happened?" Holmes demanded urgently.

"I don't know, sir, but Bates the gamekeeper has just arrived unexpected."

We found Braithwaite in his study with the gamekeeper, florid faced and stockily built, wearing rough tweeds and workmanlike boots. He carried a thumb stick favoured by Westmorland shepherds.

"Bates found this on the far side of Witch's Wood," Braithwaite explained, proffering a piece of paper to Holmes. "He thought it might be of importance."

I looked over Holmes's shoulder as he examined the paper, crumpled and discoloured as though it had lain in the open for some time. It bore the handwritten numbers 16, 21, 18, 16, 15 and 19.

"The numbers mean nothing to me, although I have been . . ." Braithwaite began, but Holmes interrupted.

"Splendid work, Bates. I am gratified one member of the household staff can act with intelligence. Is anyone else aware of your discovery?"

"No, sir. I brought it directly to Mr Braithwaite."

"Excellent," Holmes told him. "You will doubtless be asked the reason for your arrival. You are to say nothing except that you have found some important evidence and are under strict instructions from myself not to discuss it. Is that clear?"

"You can rely on me, sir." Bates touched his forelock and left us.

"Is this important then?" Braithwaite asked.

"I cannot immediately say," Holmes replied. "But once it becomes known Bates has found something of alleged significance, it may give certain persons pause for thought. His discretion is to be trusted?"

"Absolutely," Braithwaite said with conviction.

"Good," said Holmes. "Then let us consider these numbers. You say they convey nothing to you?"

"Nothing at all," said Braithwaite. "But could they be some manner of code? If they are the numbers of the letters of the alphabet, they spell PURPOS. Almost a word but what can it mean?"

"From the word 'purpose' almost anything could follow," Holmes observed. "In any event, the explanation is too facile. Only the most simple of minds would use so juvenile a code which could be unravelled in seconds and we are not dealing with villainy of low intelligence."

"Perhaps the code is more subtle then?" I suggested.

"Possibly." Holmes examined the paper, then shook his head. "We can discount seven commonly used numerical permutations, unless you can perceive any relevance in the word 'ginger' which one produces."

"May I examine it again?" Braithwaite asked and Holmes handed the paper back to him. "Could it be the scores in some game? If so then it clearly appears immaterial, and . . ."

"Cribbage!" I cried triumphantly. "We have just learned that your groom plays cribbage in the village pub. What do you think, Holmes?"

"That it is difficult to perceive a connection between a regular evening of cards over a modest glass of beer and these outrages," he commented. "In any event, Watson, your knowledge of the game is deficient. A score of nineteen is impossible in cribbage and progress is marked on a peg board, not by writing down the scores."

He smiled as I looked deflated.

"A sprightly effort, but not I think, correct. However, the possibility it is a code leads to the conclusion that more than one person is involved, one within the household and the second outside; persons working together would not need to communicate in writing."

"And why should any communication be in code?" Braithwaite asked.

"The note could have been left in the woods to be picked up later," said Holmes. "A code would mean that its discovery by another would not reveal anything. Unless of course it can be deciphered."

"Can you do that?" Braithwaite asked.

"Given sufficient time," Holmes replied. "The problem is that no more than two words could be accommodated in the message, giving little material to work from. But such brevity may be indicative of urgency which could be revealing . . . just a moment! The note again if you please."

Braithwaite handed the paper to Holmes who examined it again. "I was idle in trying only seven combinations. An eighth produces 'Kirkby'. Does that mean anything to you?"

"Kirkby Lonsdale is only a few miles away, near the Yorkshire border," said Braithwaite.

"A meeting place?" Holmes suggested. "Our arrival will have given the culprits cause for concern. A village some miles away would be suitable for a council of war. We will visit Kirkby Lonsdale, Watson and see if there are reports of strangers in the vicinity."

"We can scarcely knock on every door," I objected.

"If you were to meet someone in a small village, where would you choose as a trysting place? The church? The local public house? Outside a municipal building? The choices are restricted. Tomorrow we leave for Kirkby and in the meantime Bates will say he has presented us with something undefined but of importance and we may indicate that the net is closing."

"You hope to trick the culprits into some hasty indiscretion," Braithwaite commented.

"Precisely," said Holmes. "We only have a signpost to Kirkby. Our visit will not necessarily produce the answers we seek."

As we waited for Braithwaite in the study before dinner that evening, Holmes was silent and absorbed in thought.

"I do not relish forcing the pace, Watson," he announced suddenly. "But I have no choice. Did you see *The Times* today?"

"Only very briefly."

"There was a report from Marseilles concerning a murder in that city. When Braithwaite brought this mystery to us, I had been urgently engaged for some time on serious matters and only a temporary lull in certain proceedings allowed me to accommodate him. But I must return to London within the next few days."

"Can this mystery be resolved in that time?" I asked.

"I pray so," he replied. "It has been a strain for me to take on this case and I fear I may not have been at the peak of my form. This matter is terrible for Braithwaite and his sister, but if I fail in what I am engaged in elsewhere it will be terrible for half the civilised world."

"Then return to London immediately," I suggested. "I will continue here as best I can."

"And a good best it would be," he said with a quiet smile. "But there is no need yet. I have made certain arrangements which mean I will be summoned instantly should the need arise."

Braithwaite's arrival prevented me from questioning him further, but his sombre and doom-laden mood remained with me.

Holmes deliberately turned to our host at dinner as Painter, assisted by one of the maids, was serving the meal.

"Watson and I will need two horses tomorrow," he said. "I must make enquiries which I am certain will bring me to the solution."

I noticed a look of interest cross Painter's face. Holmes's request would quickly become common knowledge in the household.

"That should suffice," Holmes remarked as the servants left us. "It will be interesting to see what results it may produce."

We left early the following day and rode over the Devil's Bridge into Kirkby Lonsdale at noon. We went to the principal tavern for luncheon, where Holmes engaged the landlord in conversation. Encouraged by my friend's questions about fishing, the publican became increasingly forthcoming, their conversation interrupted only by his greeting every customer by name.

"You know your clientele well," Holmes remarked.

"After sixteen years I should do, sir," the man replied. "There are few people who walk through that door who are strangers to me. You're the first I've not known for a twelvemonth."

"Remarkable," said Holmes. "However, we must be on our way, landlord. Thanks for your hospitality."

As we walked away, Holmes shook his head. "That was clearly not the meeting place. We must divide our forces. You go to the church while I make enquiries elsewhere. We are seeking the presence, within the past few days, of a man and a woman, unknown to the villagers."

"A man and a woman. How can you be certain?"

"Braithwaite and his sister each saw the woman and the accomplice is not likely to be other than a man I think. Meet me back here in two hours."

My own enquiries were fruitless. I found the verger but he afforded me nothing, then I chanced upon an elderly woman — clearly the village gossip — whose cottage overlooked the old Norman church. It was clear that the vantage point of her home meant no stranger could have been in the vicinity of St Mary's without her being aware. I was treated to a detailed account of everything that had occurred in the area during the past several weeks before I was able to excuse myself. Returning to the rendezvous point with Holmes, I hoped he had enjoyed more success, but the look on his face when I saw him approaching dashed my hopes.

"My trail is cold, Watson," he announced grimly. "You do not give the appearance of a man who has enjoyed any more success."

"All I have learned is that on the fourteenth a travelling circus passed through the town," I replied. "Otherwise there are no reports of any strangers in the . . ."

Holmes slapped the heel of his hand against his forehead. "What an imbecile I have been!"

"What do you mean?"

"Just because a line of reasoning is ingenious, Watson,

does not mean that it must be right," he replied. "But its cleverness flatters our conceit and we are in danger of closing our minds to the truth because it is, by comparison, pedestrian. My ingenuity — of which you frequently speak so warmly — has prevented me from observing the simple. We must return to Meldred Hall."

"But I cannot see . . ." I began.

"Neither could I, Watson," he interrupted. "When you are seeking the needle, you must first ensure you are looking in the right haystack."

As we rode back, I was at a loss to understand how Holmes could suddenly be so satisfied, but he remained uncommunicative and I could not untangle the knot for myself.

Johnson hurried out to meet us as we reached Meldred Hall shortly after seven o'clock.

"Mr Holmes! You must go to the Hall immediately."

"What has happened?" Holmes demanded.

"The Firewitch has struck again!"

Holmes leapt from his horse. "Your master and Miss Eleanor. Pray God they have come to no further harm!"

"They are both well, sir," Johnson assured him. "It was one of the maids she attacked."

"What new mischief is this?" Holmes muttered as we ran from the stables to where Braithwaite was waiting on the front steps.

"It's Alice McGregor," he said in answer to Holmes's questioning look. "She was attacked this afternoon."

"By the bird?"

"No, by Mad Meg, a simpleton of the village. The girl can tell you everything."

He took us to the servants' wing at the rear of the house, where McGregor was being tended by Mrs Broom. The edge of a bruise was visible beneath a bandage applied to the maid's head. Despite her injury, she was able to tell Holmes what had occurred.

"I'd gone out to feed the poultry," she said. "As I was returning, Mad Meg appeared in front of me and struck me with her stick. As I fell, I heard her say she was the Firewitch."

"What were her precise words?"

The girl thought for a moment. "'The Firewitch will have you all'."

Holmes glanced at Braithwaite. "Has this woman been located?"

"The police have gone to her cottage in Attwater, but she is nowhere to be found. I have told them to bring her here as soon as they can."

"Very well," said Holmes, then he turned back to the girl in the bed. "You must rest. You have been very brave."

Downstairs Holmes spoke to other members of the staff. None of them had seen Mad Meg near the house that day, but said she was a frequent visitor, begging for food or old clothing. When he had finished, my friend was alone with Painter for some time.

"Almost there, Watson," he remarked as he rejoined me in the sitting-room. "We will now await the apprehension of Mad Meg."

He warmed his hands at the fire. "Have you observed how chilly it is in the servants' quarters?" After this runic remark he said no more, but there was a gleam of satisfaction in his eyes.

Some three hours later, a police sergeant and constable brought Mad Meg to the Hall. The pitiful creature was well named, dressed in the foulest rags with lank hair falling about her wrinkled face. Her eyes stared wildly about the kitchen where all the staff were gathered. Her dribbling mouth twitched as she mumbled incoherently, gnarled fingers twisting some wild flowers she had picked. From my medical knowledge, I felt certain we would get no sense out of her.

"So this is the Firewitch," Holmes said reflectively. "What can you tell me of her, sergeant?"

"A local idiot, Mr Holmes. Mad Meg's lived in these parts all her life. She's backward, but up to now has been harmless. She wanders about chattering away to herself, talking to the birds and the like. It seems her mind has taken a turn for the worse."

He looked at us significantly. "There's talk in Attwater that she claims to have been visited by the spirit of Margaret Seymour and has been given her powers."

"Most conclusive," Holmes nodded approvingly. "May I suggest she be confronted by her latest victim?"

"Exactly my thinking, sir," the man replied enthusiastically. "If the poor lass is up to it."

"Our presence will reassure her she is in no danger."

Alice McGregor, led into the kitchen on the arm of a solicitous Mrs Broom, recoiled in terror when she saw the madwoman.

"Do not be afraid," said Holmes. "Is this the woman who attacked you?"

"Yes," the girl replied timidly.

Mad Meg glowered malevolently, then suddenly spat.

"God help me!" Alice screamed, frantically rubbing her bodice where the spittle had landed. "The Firewitch has cursed me!"

"That's enough!" the sergeant cried. "Don't you worry, young woman, no harm will come to you now."

As Mrs Broom comforted the sobbing McGregor, the officers pulled Mad Meg to her feet. Holmes stepped across the room and stood in front of her for a moment then bent down and looked closely at her wizened face.

"Do your duty, sergeant," he said. "It is a sad business, but the law must decide if this woman's mental condition places her outside its restrictions. Meldred Hall need have no further fear."

"But what about the bird?" asked Braithwaite.

"The sergeant has already answered that," Holmes replied. "Mad Meg has a reputation of talking to the birds and who knows what rare and unsuspected powers of control her strange mind may have over them? There are buzzards in this neighbourhood and all hunting birds can be trained. Am I not right, sergeant?"

"Absolutely, sir." The man looked pleased. "Always had a way with animals has Mad Meg."

As the wretched woman was led away, Holmes turned to Braithwaite. "You see, nothing supernatural, just a degenerate madwoman who had become dangerous. You must tell your sister of the conclusion of this matter. Watson and I will await you."

Holmes and I left the kitchen and went to Braithwaite's study where my companion closed the door firmly behind us.

"That woman may make no better sense in the morning," he remarked. "But at least she may be more amenable when the effects of the drink so evident on her breath have subsided. What a fine old farce we have been witness to!"

"Then Mad Meg is not the culprit?" I exclaimed.

"Watson, do not disappoint me," Holmes said impatiently. "This tarradiddle may fool the police and the local incredulous, but surely you are not deceived as well?"

"It has some persuasive factors. If they locate this buzzard . . ."

"There is no buzzard," Holmes interrupted dismissively. "That was only my contribution to this deception. However, we must maintain the appearance of having been misled by a scheme devised specifically for our benefit. Braithwaite alone we can take into our confidence."

A few moments later our host rejoined us. "Mr Holmes, I have spoken to my sister, but I am far from satisfied at this stage that . . ."

"Of course you are not satisfied," said Holmes. "Our intelligence has been insulted by this ridiculous act of desperation concocted to deflect me from my purpose. Virtually the entire picture is now clear. Just a little more information, and I know where to look for it. Advise Painter that Watson and I will be leaving for London in the morning, our business here having been completed."

"London?" Braithwaite cried. "How is the answer there?"

"It is not," said Holmes. "And neither shall we be. We shall leave the train at Manchester, and return as soon as possible. Can you advise us of a small inn within a few miles of here — to the west, by the by — where we might pass ourselves off as innocent visitors? With false names, we should not be recognised."

Braithwaite suggested a suitable place and Holmes took directions as to how we could reach it.

"That appears ideal," he said. "Watson, I must ask you to take on the guise of a naturalist who has come to the Lake District to catalogue the early spring flowers. Braithwaite, expect to hear from me by the post. I cannot say when, but you must carry out any instructions it contains absolutely. To quote a distinguished son of these parts, we have gone from a find to a check and now may proceed to a view and a kill."

He gazed into the fire, a look of keen anticipation on his face.

"However, perhaps we might pass our time discussing legal matters. As one of Her Majesty's Crown Prosecutors, you must have been involved in several cases in which I would find points of interest."

Looking rather surprised, our host agreed, and for the rest of the evening Holmes asked about Braithwaite's career, without making any reference to the matters which had brought us to Meldred Hall.

THE DOOM OF THE GREAT BIRD

"Rumour will now be our ally, Watson," Holmes gestured out of the carriage window as our train pulled out of Oxenholme the following morning. "Word of Mad Meg's arrest will spread like a bushfire and her guilt unquestionably concluded. After all, the great Sherlock Holmes is satisfied she was the Firewitch, so what other suspicions can remain?"

I did not question him further. It was invariably my friend's habit to be elliptical when on the brink of the solution to a mystery, while still lacking the absolute proof of the concluding details.

In Manchester we bought suitably rustic clothes in the city's Oxford Street, then made our way to the nearby University where we obtained some basic scientific equipment and reference books to give credence to our intended roles. Holmes also purchased a pair of powerful binoculars. Camouflaged by our disguise, we returned north from the capital of King Cotton and installed ourselves in the small, but clean and comfortable Lyth Valley Inn in the shadow of the peaks westward of Meldred Hall. Our works of English flora and specimen boxes seemed to satisfy the landlord and his wife that we were indeed researchers of natural history and we set off the following morning filled with advice as to where several rare species of plants might be found.

"Our paths divide here, Watson," Holmes announced as we left the tiny hamlet and reached a stream chuckling over rocks. "You must continue and collect enough specimens to support our story. I will meet you at the tavern this evening."

He forded the shallow stream and struck off in the direction of the hills ahead of us. I watched his tall figure rising up the greensward until it was almost invisible then began my duties as an imitation botanist. By the afternoon, I had collected a fair number of samples and made my way back to the inn in the early evening. Holmes had still not returned and I was sitting in the warmth of the tiny snug bar when he arrived. He asked the landlady if she could provide him with a meal then brought his ale and joined me on the oak settle by the fireside.

"The lady is most impressed with what you have collected," he remarked with a grin. "You have quite hoaxed her. I have been equally successful, but have nothing tangible I can display. But I found what I was seeking in the mountains. I have also discovered a route to Meldred Hall that avoids the road."

"Have you been there? To the Hall?"

"Only to observe it from a distance," he replied. "Then I found a village which boasts a small post office from where I was able to write to Braithwaite. The trap closes, Watson, and there will be no escape."

We quitted our accommodation next morning, announcing our intention of going further towards the coast, but instead made our way up into the mountains. Holmes showed me the shepherd's tracks he had discovered the previous day and soon we were high over the wide, flat valley with Meldred Hall faintly visible in the distance. Holmes stopped at one point and directed his binoculars towards the Hall.

"Braithwaite has done his work," he commented but did not explain how he knew that to be the case.

We descended to the level pasture land and another hour's walk took us past the mere by Lowman's Farm and into Witch's Wood. We pitched camp at the edge of a clearing in the undergrowth and ate the food we had purchased from the inn prior to our departure. In the late afternoon we heard someone approaching through the trees.

"Mr Holmes?" a voice whispered and moments later Braithwaite appeared through the bushes at the edge of the clearing.

"Over here," Holmes called softly and Braithwaite joined us in the protective cover of dead bracken. "You have done exactly what I asked?"

"Yes, although it has caused my household immense distress. That I should be selling Meldred Hall and dismissing more than half of them at such short notice has appalled them. Mrs Broom was in tears and my heart ached to comfort her by explaining it was all a ruse of your devising."

"I am relieved that you controlled your tenderer feelings," Holmes said drily. "They must all believe without question that you are serious. They are all aware of your apparent intentions?"

"I called the entire household and stable staff to my study this morning," Braithwaite replied. "I had Bates the gamekeeper brought to the hall for the meeting. Only the tenant farmers remain to be informed."

"And at what time did you say you were leaving the Hall this evening to do that?" Holmes asked.

"I told Painter I would set off at seven o'clock to go straight to Lowman's Farm first then on to the others. Doubtless he will have told the other staff."

"And what of your sister?" Holmes enquired.

"I have said she is aware of my plans but they are on no account to mention it to her in her present condition."

"Excellent," Holmes said. "Do not concern yourself over what will happen next. We will both be with you, even if you cannot see us."

There was a sharp frost that evening and I was glad we had bought substantial woollen clothing while in Manchester; lighting a fire was out of the question. As darkness fell, we made our way to the edge of the woods and crouched in the bushes, peering in the direction towards which Meldred Hall lay. Just after six o'clock, a figure I could not recognise hurried past in the gloom within yards of our hiding place.

"The bait is taken, Watson," Holmes breathed.

An hour later we heard the sound of hooves and a glimmer of light appeared, bouncing up and down in the blackness. As we watched, the shadowy figure of Braithwaite and his horse trotted past, flitteringly lit by the shining lantern fastened to his saddle. We crept out and followed him and I was grateful for my army experience as we proceeded with infinite caution, keeping some hundred yards behind. I carried my old service revolver in my hand. Braithwaite rode through and out of the woods until he was skirting the mere, a mirror of cold silver in the white moonlight. It was eerily silent as we followed, falling further behind as our cover lessened and we waited in each clump of bushes to ensure that the coast was clear before moving swiftly to the next hiding place. Suddenly we saw a burst of orange flame rise from the undergrowth beside the horseman ahead of us.

"Quickly, Watson! We have them!" Holmes cried and we began to run.

The light was a blazing torch which its bearer, indistinguishable in the darkness, thrust into the face of Braithwaite's horse. The animal whinnied and reared, throwing its rider to the ground. Immediately, the figure leapt upon him as Holmes shouted a warning, then I tripped on something and brought Holmes down with me as I fell. As we scrambled to our feet again, the figure hurled the torch to one side and dashed away along the edge of the mere. We raced on towards Braithwaite then my blood and body froze as some huge bird, larger than anything I had ever seen, swooped silently and terribly across the still waters of the lake and landed on his inert form.

"Your revolver, Watson! Shoot, for the love of God!" Holmes shouted.

I raised the weapon, but in the gloom the squirming turmoil of screaming man and screeching bird was too confused to risk an immediate shot. As I ran on, I heard the hoot of an owl. Immediately the bird rose, hovered above its victim for a moment, then swept back over the mere. In the blackness it was immense and hideous and I could clearly see two great curved horns rising from its head against the cold light of the moon. In a great emotion of rage, I raised my gun again and blasted away at the loathsome apparition. By some chance — I take no credit for any marksmanship in the situation — one bullet found its target. The bird squawked and spun round then crumpled and fell like a broken kite into the freezing waters below. From the far side of the water came a howl of anguish.

Holmes was crouching over Braithwaite as I rushed up to them. Down the side of his face was a savage cut, deeper than the gashes caused by the talons of the bird.

"Thank God, he is not seriously hurt," Holmes said. "He is a brave man indeed to have risked himself that this devilry might be exposed."

He looked across the lake to where a dark mass of feathers

was floating, concentric circles of ripples spreading across the shining water towards the shore.

"A notable shot, Watson," he commented. "That abused and dangerous creature had to be destroyed."

"Pure chance," I said. "But what of its human agents?"

"They will not get far. I shall ride back on Braithwaite's horse and sound the alarm. Attend to him until I return with assistance."

"But who are they?" I demanded as he rose to leave.

"The so-called Alice McGregor and her brother," he replied as he mounted into the saddle. "They were enacting a terrible revenge for a dead man."

BROTHER AND SISTER

Holmes returned with Painter and Johnson the groom and together we carried Braithwaite back to Meldred Hall. While I treated his wounds — the cut was deep, but the rest little more than superficial, the bird having retreated within seconds of striking — word reached us that farmer Lowman, aroused by my shots, had hurried out and found Alice McGregor and her brother trying to take two of his horses. He and his two sturdy sons had taken them captive and were holding them until they received further information. Holmes ordered that they should be kept secure and brought to Meldred Hall in the morning when the police would be called.

Shortly after dawn, the stable lad was dispatched to Kendal for the constabulary and Holmes instructed Johnson to retrieve the remains of the bird from the mere. He returned with Lowman, his shotgun pointed at the guilty couple. Alice McGregor was dressed in shabby rags and her face was streaked with dirt; she had made herself look artificially old with theatrical make-up. Her brother, some years her senior, was a sour-looking bearded individual, face narrow and furtive, wearing what had once been a gentleman's Norfolk jacket.

Holmes turned his attention first to the bird which Johnson had laid in the yard outside the kitchen. The groom had also brought a wooden cage which he had discovered — as Holmes had suggested — near the edge of the lake.

"A golden eagle." Holmes knelt down and removed the sodden leather hood with the horns of a ram attached which had been fixed to its head. "A noble bird used for an ignoble deed."

We went back into the Hall where Braithwaite was in the sitting-room with his sister who had insisted on being present. Holmes told Lowman to bring the criminals in.

"There is your bird of the Firewitch," he told Braithwaite grimly, showing him the hood. "Trained to attack at the smell of blood by this man in a crime planned with his sister."

"But Alice McGregor has been . . ." Braithwaite began. Holmes held up his hand and interrupted him.

"Not Alice McGregor," he corrected. "Alice Fleming and her brother Duncan, next of kin of Stuart Fleming, the murderer who was executed in Carlisle four years ago after you led for the prosecution."

He swung towards the couple standing before us with heads bowed.

"Do you dispute this? Then your silence confirms it." He turned back to Braithwaite. "When I learned in our conversation the other evening that it was among your cases, the last pieces of the puzzle fell into place. When you first told me of this strange great bird, I wondered if it was some exotic species with a large crest resembling horns in the darkness. An examination of the reference books in your library contained nothing in world ornithology that fitted and then my mind turned to other possibilities. The largest bird in these islands is the great golden eagle, most commonly found in Scotland. Even then I did not see my way clearly until I remembered that this Scotswoman who called herself Alice McGregor joined your household three years ago. When you told me Fleming was one of a large family, the picture became complete.

"These two planned to have their vengeance on you for your part in their brother's conviction. The first stage was when she came to Meldred Hall and would have learned the story of the Attwater Firewitch and together they hatched this diabolical scheme. Fleming here must have taken an eaglet from its nest in the Highlands and trained it as it grew to maturity. It would attack anything that smelled of blood but would return when he gave the signal — the hoot of an owl, which you, Miss Braithwaite, heard just before you fainted.

"Nothing could be done until the bird was trained, which is why the so-called Alice McGregor remained as a satisfactory servant for the period that would take. Then Fleming himself moved to the district, living rough somewhere in the foothills of the mountains. My enquiries among the hill shepherds revealed that they had seen an eagle in recent months. The cage was his means of transporting it to the woods.

"The disappearance of whisky from your decanter — for which the luckless Adams was blamed — was also the work of this woman. Apart from a Scotsman's natural affinity for the drink, it would have been of great assistance to her brother as he lived out in the winter cold."

As Holmes was speaking, I observed increasingly resentful and bitter looks filling the faces of the guilty brother and sister.

"All the attacks of the bird had to be preceded by the victim being brought into contact with blood," my companion continued. "In the case of your dog, some creature had been left in the grass — a rabbit perhaps — to which it ran when it caught the scent. Fleming then released the bird and it killed the dog in order to get the original prey. In the other instances, Alice always struck first, leaving blood on your faces. In your case, Braithwaite, she adopted the legendary manner of the Firewitch in her cell. The blood she held in her mouth was from the self-inflicted cut on her hand, explained as the result of an accidental fall. Your sister, she struck with a bramble."

Braithwaite looked at the couple with revulsion.

"But why did they call the bird off?" he said. "They could have left it to kill either of us."

"I do not pretend to understand their minds fully," Holmes replied. "There are dark sides to many human souls comprehensible only to those whose bodies they inhabit. Anyone capable of planning and executing such a crime will be irrational in other of their attitudes."

Eleanor Braithwaite leaned forward in her chair.

"Alice, look at me," she said softly. The woman raised her eyes sullenly. "In this house you have received nothing but kindness. How could you do this dreadful thing to us?"

The servant's face flared with hatred.

"What kindness did this man show in that courtroom?" she cried, pointing at Braithwaite. "Our brother was hanged because of what he said that day. He had no mercy then and we can never forgive him."

"He was carrying out his duty as a Crown Prosecutor under the law," Holmes said sternly. "Your brother was rightly convicted of the murder of a defenceless man in pursuit of theft and deserved his fate. You cannot set yourself above such things."

"Love is above such things," the woman replied defiantly. "And we loved our brother."

"I love my brother," Eleanor Braithwaite responded gallantly. "But if he were guilty of a wicked crime then I also would have to condemn him."

"Then heaven help you for a heartless . . ."

"Enough!" cried Holmes. "You will not compound your iniquity with insults against this lady in my presence. Deliver them to the police, Lowman." He watched the pair leave the room, then turned to Eleanor Braithwaite. "I was not happy about you being present this morning. There was no need for you to face such creatures."

"I cannot comprehend her," she replied, shaking her head. "Of what manner of love does she speak?"

Holmes shrugged. "It is among the emotions to which I am a stranger, but I have had occasion to observe its power more than once. And it has been my conclusion that love destroys as often as it blesses. In this instance, we can only conclude that their feelings for their brother led them to want to extend their own sense of suffering to you both, not by causing your deaths but by perhaps driving you to madness."

Holmes's face, which had grown very grim, took on a sudden smile.

"However, it is now over and you can advise your staff, Braithwaite, that you intend to continue living here with them all around you."

"There will be great joy when they hear it," he replied feelingly. "But why did you wish me to suggest that I was leaving?"

"When Alice McGregor heard she was to be dismissed, I calculated that she and her brother would arrange one final — probably murderous — attack. I told you to give all of them a day's liberty after breaking the news, which would allow her time to communicate with him and make the arrangements. Then it only remained for you to announce your intention of riding to Lowman's Farm in the evening and the trap was set. I was satisfied that the presence of Watson and myself would ensure your safety. I greatly regret that we were not able to reach you before the bird actually struck."

"My injuries are nothing compared to my sense of relief," Braithwaite assured him. "If you will excuse us, I will summon my staff."

Eleanor Braithwaite left the room with her brother and a short while later we heard a cheer from the direction of the study.

"And Johnson the groom was quite uninvolved," I remarked.

"As much as poor Mad Meg," Holmes replied. "They faked the attack by her, in which Fleming must have struck his own sister, to deflect suspicion when I announced I was nearing the solution."

"And the paper that Bates discovered was irrelevant," I commented.

"On the contrary, it was of critical importance," said Holmes, "although the suggestion that it was a code led me in the wrong direction when my own ingenuity deceived me. By chance, the word 'Kirkby' could be unravelled from the numbers and I was immediately persuaded that was the path to follow. Only when you told me that there had been a passing circus in the town on the fourteenth of the month did I realise that the numbers were simply dates. In fact they are the dates in each month since last October which Painter later advised me were Alice Fleming's days off. I knew that it was Braithwaite's practice to give his staff a day off each month because Mrs Johnson said she and her husband visited his relations in Kendal on his. Alice must have written down her free days and given the paper to her brother who inadvertently lost it in the woods.

"Remember also something that Mrs Broom told us. On the afternoon Eleanor Braithwaite was attacked, Alice begged for additional time off. She did not of course visit friends, but perpetrated the attack upon Miss Braithwaite."

"But how did she communicate with her brother on that occasion?" I asked. "He would not have expected her to be available until her next day's leave."

"You will remember that her room is at the rear of the house," Holmes replied. "When we saw her there after the alleged attack by Mad Meg — another occasion when she had to summon her brother unexpectedly of course — you may have observed that the room was singularly cold. I commented on the fact to you later. As on previous occasions, she had left her window wide open for most of the day, a visible signal to anyone in the mountains using a telescope, just as Johnson watches passing ships looking in the opposite direction towards the coast.

"As we made our way here, Watson, you will remember that I stopped to look at Meldred Hall through the binoculars. As I had anticipated, the window of her room was open again and I knew Braithwaite had carried out my instructions and his intentions had been believed."

Braithwaite and his sister invited us to stay at Meldred Hall for as long as we wished, but Holmes insisted he must return to London.

"This case has meant that I have had to allow other most urgent matters to go unattended," he told them. "While I have been away, a certain Professor of my acquaintance will not have been idle."

He spoke lightly, but now, as I mourn my greatest friend and one of the most remarkable men England ever bore, I constantly reproach myself for not being more alert to the ultimate danger he was facing. On the twenty-fourth of the following month he asked me to accompany him on that fateful journey to the Continent. The mystery of the Attwater Firewitch was his last investigation before the final, deadly encounter with Moriarty at the Reichenbach Falls.

Chapter Eight

It was half past one before Maltravers turned off the light and lay in the darkness, the spell of *The Attwater Firewitch* fading to be replaced by the returning, tantalising facts surrounding Charles Carrington's murder. Faced with such a case, Holmes would have made some runic comment about an apparently irrelevant scrap of evidence and later demonstrated how it solved everything: "*I draw your attention to the curious incident of . . .*" Maltravers told himself he was being fanciful and went to sleep.

In the morning his half-awake mind dangled an idea in front of his consciousness. He stared at the bedroom ceiling, trying to piece it together like fragments of a dream, then sat up abruptly and grabbed the manuscript, flicking through it urgently. After a few moments he lowered the pages and smiled.

"Could that really be it? If it is, thank you, Sherlock." He leapt out of bed, pulled on his dressing gown and hurried downstairs to the kitchen where Lucinda was preparing breakfast and Malcolm was opening the post.

"Where's Jennifer?" Maltravers asked.

"She'll be down in a minute," Lucinda replied. "What are you so excited about?"

Maltravers held up *The Attwater Firewitch*. "I think I know the code for that safe." He turned to Malcolm, staring at him with a half-opened envelope in his hands. "Have you ever read this?"

"No. I was going to when you'd finished. Why?"

"Look here." Maltravers put the photocopy on the table as Jennifer Carrington entered the room. "Good. I won't have to explain this twice."

He pointed to a paragraph. "One of the clues Holmes solves in this involves a series of numbers. There are six of them, but isn't it possible that Charles used the first four for the safe combination? He'd have had to choose something."

They looked at the passage he was indicating.

"Which means that if he did . . ." Malcolm paused as he began to grasp it for himself.

"Which means that only someone who had read the book would have been able to try these numbers." Maltravers waited for them to catch up.

"I don't understand. Is this important?" Jennifer Carrington appeared confused.

"It could be critical," Maltravers told her. "If I'm right, it's a very damning piece of evidence against Duggie Lydden. The night Charles showed me this book, Lydden admitted he was one of the people who'd read it. Which means he could have guessed the combination and tried it."

"What should we do?" Jennifer asked, looking again at the numbers as though still unable to grasp their significance.

"I thought of going to Carwelton Hall and testing them for myself," said Maltravers. "But if I'm wrong, off goes the alarm, someone calls the police and they get tetchy. Tempting though it is, I think I'd better go straight to them with it."

"Can I come with you?"

"Give me five minutes to get dressed."

In Kendal police station, they were taken straight through to Moore after Maltravers had explained the reason for their visit. The sergeant listened carefully, then asked to examine the photocopy himself.

"How did you work this out?" he asked.

"I have nothing to confess but my genius," Maltravers replied. "But I'm quite prepared to be exposed as an idiot when you try it."

"It's certainly worth trying." Moore looked up at him and smiled. "I take it you'd like to be there."

"Very much." Having had more time to think, Maltravers had become determined to find a way of being present when the police operated the dial; he wanted to see Jennifer Carrington's reaction. Moore followed them in his own car to Carwelton Hall.

"I've advised the safe makers to ignore any alarms from here in the next half-hour," Moore said as he consulted the photocopy in the library. "We don't want unnecessary panics. Right, first four numbers."

He took hold of the dial and began to turn it. "Sixteen . . . twenty-one . . . eighteen . . . and back to sixteen."

There was a rattle of tumblers then Moore pushed down the handle and pulled the door open. Jennifer Carrington reached forward and touched it in disbelief. Maltravers had placed himself so he could see her face and visible triumph flickered across it and vanished. Triumph over what?

"Congratulations, Mr Maltravers," Moore said appreciatively. "First you point out the problem, then you solve it. We'll need another statement from you of course."

"I expected that." Maltravers was still watching Jennifer, but her face was now immobile. "But it opens up more possibilities as well, doesn't it? I know Duggie Lydden had read the book, but so had others."

"So I understand. Do you know any of them, Mrs Carrington?"

"Pardon?" Moore's question seemed to startle her. "I'm not sure. Stephen Campbell and Dr Bryant and some others, but I don't know all their names."

"I can add another," said Maltravers. "Alan Morris, the vicar of Attwater. He told me so."

"Alan?" Jennifer Carrington shook her head in rejection. "But he's like Stephen and Dr Bryant. Nobody could suspect him. Surely the point is that Duggie had read it."

"We'll need everyone you can remember," Moore told her. "We have to eliminate them. Can you both follow me back to the station, please?"

He closed the safe again and they returned to their cars. As they drove back along the main road to Kendal, Jennifer glanced towards the lane leading to Attwater.

"He can't be serious about people like Alan Morris, can he? Or Stephen. It's ridiculous."

"There's a number of fish in the net apart from Lydden," Maltravers said. "They're going to have to check them all out."

At the time neither of them knew that the case against Lydden had already hardened. The police had spent all of Friday at his house on a still uncompleted estate on the outskirts of Kendal, examining loose floorboards, probing among the rafters. They had searched the garden looking for freshly disturbed earth, stripped the garage, even drained the water tank in the roof, but had found nothing. Then men with dogs had started covering the rest of the site.

Late in the afternoon one of the dogs had begun to sniff excitedly at the unfinished floor of a house about two hundred yards from Lydden's. When its handler lay down and stretched his arm as far as he could beneath the floor cavity, his fingers touched something which moved slightly. Several boards were pulled up to reveal a double barrelled shotgun with the initials DKL engraved on a brass plate on the stock. Lydden had identified it as his. With mounting evidence to support Jennifer Carrington's story of having been in Manchester all day, Lambert had authorised her release and applied for authority to hold Lydden for a further twelve hours when his initial twenty-four expired, taking him to one o'clock on Saturday afternoon.

Forensic tests had proved that the hidden shotgun had killed Charles Carrington. Lydden, whose fingerprints were the only ones on the gun, continued to deny the murder or know how the gun had got where the police had found it. The major problem Lambert and his team had been left with was the question of the safe combination, and now Maltravers was handing them the answer on a plate. After Moore had reported to him, Lambert went to see Maltravers and Jennifer Carrington himself. He fired a series of sharp questions, then Maltravers saw the satisfaction on his face as he left the room, his massive bulk just squeezing through the doorway.

"I don't have time for amateurs normally," Lambert remarked when Moore joined him again. "They're usually as much use as a sick headache. But that Maltravers has got a sight more nous than the average Londoner. I think he's just given us what we needed."

"Do we charge Lydden then? It looks like it's worth a run."

Lambert rubbed his hand across his mouth, twisting rubbery lips into a grotesque shape.

"Not yet," he said cautiously. "I'll apply for a special magistrates court to hold him for another sixty hours. That gives us time to talk to anyone else who's read that book. In the meantime we'll let Lydden stew. But unless something unexpected happens, I think we'll be hauling him up at the regular court on Monday morning and charging him. Take those names from her statement and get on with it."

Lambert's face folded in a grimace of contentment as Moore walked out. His faint reservations about Lydden's guilt in the light of repeated, angry denials were rapidly fading. Nothing had emerged to support his story for the day of the murder and, while that collapsed, evidence to prove his guilt had mounted up. Admittedly, Maltravers's explanation about the safe combination meant that other people could have known it — but they were not the owners of the murder weapon and had not been caught with the stolen goods in their house. Lambert rang the Clerk to Kendal magistrates to request a special court so he could apply to hold his suspect pending further enquiries; he felt they were academic, but the police had to go through the motions.

"Behold the detective marvel of the age." Maltravers grinned at Malcolm and Lucinda from the steps into the kitchen. He turned his face through ninety degrees before lowering his head, presenting the top of it to them. "Full face, profile and plan."

"I take it the combination worked?" Malcolm said drily.

"O ye of little faith." Maltravers crossed to where packets of cereal were still on the kitchen table; his breakfast had gone by the board earlier, although Malcolm and Lucinda had eaten. "It was a brilliant dénouement executed in the library in the best tradition."

"What did the police think of it?" Lucinda asked.

Maltravers filled a bowl and added milk and brown sugar. "My reward will probably arrive in the morning post. I have the impression they've got more on Lydden than they're letting on and the combination could clinch it — although we're still left with the question of Jennifer being in it with him."

"You still think that's possible?"

"Yes." He chewed thoughtfully on a mouthful of muesli. "There was something about her reaction when Moore opened that safe. She looked too satisfied."

"She would do," Malcolm argued. "It proved Duggie Lydden could have opened it, which was the problem."

"But it also meant somebody else could have done. Somebody else who must have read that book — which isn't many people. I know Lydden isn't bright, but if Jennifer was in it with him, why didn't he just blow the whole thing when she double-crossed him? He might not have been able to prove anything, but he could make life difficult for her. Instead, we have this story about meeting her at lunchtime. So colour him stupid, but the more I learn about all this, the more I'm convinced there's someone very clever behind it."

"Like you of course." Lucinda grinned. "We're very impressed about that code."

"Put your admiration on hold. I have the uneasy feeling I could have missed something."

In the living-room, Malcolm noticed *The Attwater Firewitch*, which Maltravers had dropped on to the settee when he came back.

"Didn't the police want to keep this?" he asked as he picked it up.

"They've got the books so the photocopy isn't vital. I told Moore I hadn't finished it. I knew you wanted to read it."

Maltravers sat on the chesterfield with that week's edition of the *Cumbrian Chronicle*. After a few minutes he looked across at Malcolm, who had started to read. Faintly in his mind was a suggestion, and the most curious thing was that he kept thinking of Sherlock Holmes. The notion faded as he pursued it and he went back to improving his scanty knowledge of the activities of the Lakeland livestock market.

Moore reported back to Lambert that afternoon. "This link between the safe combination and the book, sir. Mrs Carrington can only name five people who've read it apart from Lydden. One is Carrington's partner, a respectable lawyer who was in court all Thursday afternoon. Another bloke's been in bed with a temperature of a hundred and two for a week. That leaves . . ." He flicked over a page of his notebook. "Charlotte Quinn, who found the body, and the Reverend Morris at Attwater. The fifth is a member of the Conan Doyle Society who returned it this week. He was at a meeting in Norwich all day. After that, Carrington passed it on to Maltravers, who was reading it at the time of the murder."

Lambert's lower lip pushed out like a piece of raw liver sliding off the edge of a plate.

"Can't see it being Mrs Quinn or the vicar," he commented. "Can you?"

"No, sir," Moore replied. "Mrs Quinn was a very old friend of Carrington's—the word is she was in love with him. Drover's seeing Morris at the moment, but he doesn't look likely either. He's been the vicar of Attwater for donkey's years and has no motive we can see. And are either of them really the type to suddenly become a murderer who frames an innocent man at the same time?"

Lambert grunted in agreement. "Keep at it. We've got the names of Carrington's known friends and associates from his secretary and his personal address book. Some of them could have read the book. But unless we find someone pretty damned quick, our Mr Lydden will be charged on Monday, however much of a fuss he and his lawyer kick up."

As Moore turned to leave, Lambert stopped him then shuffled through some of the notes on his desk.

"Just a minute," he said, then picked up a piece of paper. "What about the people at the dinner party at Carrington's place? We thought one of them could have seen the safe being opened. Who was there? Lydden, Morris, this chap Maltravers, Stapleton who's the editor of the *Chronicle* and someone called Howard."

"No go," Moore replied, shaking his head. "Maltravers was absolutely certain nobody in the room could have seen. We've tried it ourselves and if everyone was standing where he says, there's no chance. Someone would have had to be at Carrington's elbow when he opened it and nobody was. It looks as though Maltravers must be right that you could only guess that code from having read the book. And that cuts out Stapleton, Maltravers at the time and Howard, who had apparently just come back from Africa. Which leaves us with Morris and Lydden. And let's face it — it really only leaves us with Lydden."

*

Alan Morris smiled as he opened the door and recognised the figure on the front step.

"Ian Drover!" he exclaimed. "I haven't seen you since . . . well not for a long time. Come in, come in."

The detective constable appeared uncomfortable as he entered the vicarage. "I'm sorry to trouble you, Mr Morris, but as you know I'm with the CID now and . . ."

"Your mother was telling me only the other week." Morris led Drover through to his study. "She's very proud of you — as we all are in Attwater. It seems no time at all since you used to come to Bible class and I remember your confirmation as though it were only yesterday. But you've not come to talk about the past. What can I do for you?"

He sat down at his desk and smiled smoothly at Drover, looking increasingly unhappy in the chair opposite.

"I'm sorry, vicar, but I'm one of the team investigating the murder of Mr Carrington and when my sergeant said we wanted to talk to you, I offered to come." He paused uncertainly. "I'm sorry, but there are some questions I must ask you."

Alan Morris leaned forward earnestly. "Questions, Ian? What about?"

"About the afternoon of the murder. We're checking on people's movements. I'm sorry, but . . ."

"Stop apologising," Morris told him sharply. "That's the fourth time you've said sorry since you arrived. You're here to do your job and the fact that I've known you all your life doesn't come into it. So you want to know what I was doing the day Mr Carrington was so tragically killed? Well immediately after lunch, I went to . . ."

Having given an account of his movements on Thursday afternoon, Morris waved to the detective constable's disappearing car with a sense of relief; another police officer might have been less accommodating. Ten minutes later, he arrived at Carwelton Hall.

"I'm sorry I couldn't come sooner," he said as Jennifer Carrington stepped back from the front door to let him enter. "The police have just been to see me about Thursday afternoon." He put his arms around her. "You must be very brave."

Chapter Nine

On Sunday morning Maltravers went into Attwater for a newspaper, then drove round narrow, twisting back lanes, rejoining the
main road near Carwelton Hall. He parked beyond the bend, then
stood by a wall, staring across low rolling fields, chill, sullen and
miserable under the dank and motionless October mist. He tried to
guess if what he could see in the distance was a crow or a rook; there
was a country legend that if you thought it was one it was always the
other and he was little better at identifying birds than cars. He was
convinced it was not a raven, as there was no bust of Pallas, pallid
or otherwise, anywhere in sight. Absently and irrelevantly, he
began to quote the poem to himself, but stumbled in verse twelve.
  "Fancy unto fancy linking," he repeated in irritation. "No,
thinking. Or is it. . . ? Oh, sod it."

  It was not just losing his way in the brooding, relentless metre of
Poe that frustrated him. Elusive and mocking, his own fancies
tormented him and he could not shake off their taunting that he
was missing things blatantly obvious. As he returned to his car in
annoyance, the jackdaw flew off across the fields.

  At the cottage, Maltravers picked up *The Attwater Firewitch*
again. Everything about the code for the safe made sense — but he
knew that — and there was nothing else that he could see. In any
case, it was preposterous to imagine that Conan Doyle's fantasy
could throw any light on a real murder a century later. Why did he
keep thinking it might? He put the book down and began to read
the views of a *Sunday Times* critic who had caught up with Tess's
play at Chester, expressing amazement that an actress of her ability
should be appearing in such second-rate dramatic tat. Maltravers
knew that the reviewer concerned had been trying unsuccessfully

to persuade anyone to stage a play of his own for several years and drew his own conclusions.

"What doth the Lord require of thee, but to do justly, and to love mercy, and to walk humbly with thy God?"

The vicar of Attwater repeated the words of the morning Lesson from the eighth verse of the sixth chapter of Micah then closed the Bible and gazed gravely round his congregation in silence for a few moments.

"Since the terrible events in this parish on Thursday, those words have been constantly with me," he said. "A dear friend of this church — a dear friend of so many of us here today — was cruelly murdered and in our grief and despair it is understandable that we feel tremendous anger against whoever was responsible for his death."

He drew himself upright. "But at such times, we must remember that God repeatedly tells us to embrace our feelings. A desire for vengeance must give way to a determination for justice. Mercy and forgiveness must temper our actions. The arrogance of judgement must be replaced with a humble acceptance of our unworthiness to judge. Love must conquer hatred, however difficult that may be."

Alan Morris leaned forward, surpliced arms resting on the edge of the pulpit. "Because when we are repulsed by another's sin, we must remember that we are all sinners. All of us, myself no less than the rest. And if we cannot find it in our hearts to forgive the sinner, then it will surely go hard with us on that dreadful day when we seek forgiveness for ourselves from the last terrible judge of all."

It was a sonorous old-fashioned sermon, rich with Biblical admonitions, delivered by a man whose own secret sins would have appalled his flock. In the front pew, with the rest of the worshippers trying not to look at her too blatantly, Jennifer Carrington sat with her hands clasped about her Prayer Book, unreadable eyes never leaving Morris's face.

Lambert reviewed the final report from the Manchester police that morning. Three of the assistants in Timperley confirmed that Mrs Carrington had arrived late in the afternoon; one said it must have been shortly before five o'clock because they had Radio One on and she had been in the shop for some time before the music was interrupted by the hourly news bulletin. Statements from the couple she had visited in the evening said she had arrived just after six o'clock and stayed for more than two hours. Lambert thrust a pudgy hand inside his jacket, produced a pen and started making notes.

Carrington had left his office in Lancaster at three fifteen; he should have reached Carwelton Hall no more than half an hour later. Charlotte Quinn had called the police at four twenty-five, having discovered the body about ten minutes earlier. Which meant . . . Lambert juggled with calculations . . . which meant that theoretically Jennifer Carrington could have returned to Carwelton Hall from Manchester in the morning, met Lydden as he claimed then waited until her husband returned and killed him with Lydden's shotgun which she had stolen earlier. Then she could have escaped before Charlotte Quinn arrived and been in Timperley by . . . Lambert scribbled through the figures. Putting aside the time she would have needed to hide the gun and put the books in Lydden's house, it was more than eighty miles in under an hour. She would have needed a Formula One racing car and to have shattered every speed limit to do it. She would also have needed to open the safe. Carrington's partner Campbell had confirmed the conversation in which Carrington had said he was the only one who knew the combination and Maltravers's statement included the fact — supported again by Campbell — that Jennifer had not read *The Attwater Firewitch*.

Abandoning the possibility as ludicrous, Lambert turned to Drover's account of his visit to Alan Morris. The vicar had been on parish business all afternoon and various witnesses broadly confirmed his movements. Unless the police very quickly learned of anybody else suspicious who had read the Conan Doyle story, being able to guess the safe combination remained a devastating piece of evidence against Duggie Lydden — among a good deal more — however much he protested.

Tess Davy was the only passenger off the train at Oxenholme just after half past four on Sunday afternoon. There was no Maltravers waiting on the platform as she carried her case through the subway and out of the exit on the other side of the line. The small car-park was empty and she looked at the bleak view of a high black stone wall directly opposite, feeling deflated and irritated after a tedious journey. Glowing in a balloon of moisture in the gloomy raw dusk, murky rays of a street lamp gleamed on the sheen of her oxblood calf-length leather coat with high-heeled black suede boots peeping below. A circular fake fur hat framed a face Raphael would have portrayed as a very worldly Madonna, although mixing the paint for her astonishing green eyes would have stretched even his creative abilities. After a few minutes she took out her purse and was looking for change for the phone box next to the exit when Maltravers's car appeared round the corner.

"Sorry," he said as he got out. "Close encounter with a wandering cow in the lane. I'll never make a rustler. Been waiting long?"

"Five minutes going on three hours," she replied as he kissed her. "The train was freezing and waiting for the connection at Warrington didn't improve matters."

"Not exactly Fun City, Western Europe," Maltravers acknowledged. "But I once saw Slough on a rainy night in February and prayed for Betjeman's friendly bombs to start falling. Come on, I'll get you to the cottage."

Tess climbed into the passenger seat, carefully folding her coat away from being caught in the door.

"What's all this about a murder up here?" she asked as Maltravers turned the car round. "There were a couple of paragraphs in the paper this morning which didn't tell me much, except that it must have happened quite nearby."

"Very," he confirmed. "And I seem to have become quite mixed up in it one way and another."

Tess listened as they drove back, a deepening frown filling her face. He finished as they pulled up outside Brook Cottage.

"And you're not satisfied are you?" she said.

"True, O Queen," he replied. "You're becoming much too good at reading my mind. There's something . . ."

Going through it all right from the beginning abruptly precipitated Maltravers's gathering frustration as phantom suggestions flitted again in the corners of his brain. Tess looked startled as he slammed his fist against the steering wheel.

"What is it, for Christ's sake? There's some stupid little thing that doesn't make sense. I *know* there is but I can't bloody well see it!"

"My God, it is getting to you, isn't it?" Tess sounded concerned. "Is it as bad as that?"

"Yes, because . . ." Maltravers paused, trying to analyse something. "Because until I can identify it, I can't convince myself that it's not important."

"But you worked out the safe combination," Tess argued. "Isn't that enough for you?"

"It should be. Malcolm and Lucinda were very impressed and the police obviously think it's important. I've got gold stars all over the place for it." Maltravers turned off the engine and they got out of the car. He looked at her across the metal roof. "But it's as though it was just waiting for someone to find it."

"Like it had been put there deliberately?" Tess suggested.

Maltravers stared at her for a moment then nodded. "I wonder if that's it? Oh, there's wisdom in women, as the poet has it."

"Do you mean knowing the combination doesn't matter?"

He shook his head. "No, it's got to matter. But perhaps not in the way we all think it does."

Tess was made welcome then went upstairs to change. In the bedroom she saw *The Attwater Firewitch* and glanced through it briefly, its presence underlining Maltravers's misgivings. She came down again wearing a Greenpeace T-shirt, jeans and white leather sandals. Shaken free from the close-fitting hat, long rippling hair glowed like dark honey filled with sunlight. Malcolm and Lucinda were in the kitchen and Maltravers was sitting in the captain's chair, one long leg hooked over the wooden arm; he appeared wrapped in the same sort of abstraction usually brought on by a new idea about something he was writing.

"Penny for them," Tess offered.

"Not worth it," he replied absently. "Not even with inflation."

"Let it go," she told him. "You're only getting uptight."

"I know I am." He sighed and stood up. "Whisky on its way."

"The trouble is that you're hung up on Sherlock Holmes," Tess said as he crossed to the cupboard in the wall and took out the bottle. "It's not really . . ."

"Of course!" Maltravers stood very still, his hand still holding the half-closed door. "The dog didn't bark in the night."

Tess looked mystified. "You haven't said anything about a dog."

Maltravers turned to face her, shaking his head impatiently. "It's just the same principle. And that means . . . just a minute, I've got to work this all out."

Tess watched as new tumbling thoughts were reflected in his face then he gave her a smile like a swallowed sun.

"What is it?" she asked.

"I've just found the needle," he announced. "I was looking in the wrong haystack. Just like Sherlock Holmes."

"The wrong haystack," Tess repeated cautiously. "Darling, what are you burbling about?"

"He's talking about *The Attwater Firewitch*." Malcolm had stepped in from the kitchen and heard the conversation. "I only know that because I've read it as well. But he's going to have to explain."

For a few moments they waited as Maltravers stood by the drinks cupboard, wrestling with his thoughts. Then he smiled again.

"But after that, of course, the dog *did* bark in the night when it shouldn't have done." He was speaking aloud to himself. "Which means . . . well, what does it mean?"

Lydden's solicitor looked uncomfortable as he faced Moore in Kendal police station.

"The police must act as they see fit, of course, but do you really have sufficient grounds to bring charges against my client?"

"Mr Lambert is satisfied," Moore told him. "There is very substantial evidence against him and we have no other suspects."

"Not at this stage," the lawyer corrected. "My client still insists that he is innocent."

"Then we'll have to see what the magistrates make of it, won't we?" Moore observed. "As far as the police are concerned, we have a case to present to them."

"Only a circumstantial one as far as I can see. I shall request an immediate dismissal and if that fails, I shall certainly make an application for bail."

"And the police will oppose you." Moore shrugged. "We've both got our jobs to do. Let's see who the magistrates agree with."

The lawyer left the room and returned to the police cell where Lydden leapt up in anticipation as he entered.

"Well?" he demanded. "Have you made them see sense?"

"They're taking you before the magistrates in the morning and will press charges of murder and other offences."

Lydden stared in outrage. "The bastards! Christ, I'll sue them when this bloody thing is over! I'll wreck that Lambert's career. I'll make him eat dirt. I'll . . ."

"Duggie," the solicitor interrupted warningly. "At the moment, all I want from you is some evidence — any evidence — that I can produce to the court in the morning. And keep your mouth shut when you appear. You're in enough trouble without shouting threats all over the place."

Lydden regarded him with disgust. "Then you can piss off. You're no bloody use to me if you think I'm guilty as well. You do, don't you?"

"You're telling me you didn't do it, Duggie," the solicitor replied. "I'll represent you as best I can, but I need some ammunition."

"Like what?"

"Frankly, like anything," the lawyer told him wearily. "I can't see that they've got enough to prove anything absolutely at the moment, but if they can cast doubts on your seeing Jennifer Carrington at Carwelton Hall on Thursday — and they've made no secret about being confident over that — then it's going to be very heavy going. And knowing that safe combination . . ."

"But I don't know it!" Lydden protested. "I read that book God knows how long ago and Charles never told me about using the numbers in it."

"Well put it this way, Duggie. It seems that whoever opened that safe knew the combination, which they could have worked out from the book. The police say they've checked everyone else who they know has read it and are satisfied they're in the clear. Any suggestions?"

Lydden turned away. The suggestion he wanted to scream was that Jennifer Carrington had virtually agreed with him that they could steal the books, if they could only find a way of opening the safe. But there had never been any question of murder in Lydden's mind. Now he did not know what was happening and was terrified of admitting something that might be forged into more evidence against himself in the face of her lies. Just one witness — anybody — who had seen him at the shop that afternoon could put him in the clear. Until that happened, he could only struggle in the web that had been woven around him. He hated Jennifer Carrington with a searing intensity; she was the only woman who had been too clever for him and he could not see how she had done it.

Tess, Malcolm and Lucinda remained silent as Maltravers finished. As he looked round at them all, they appeared dubious.

"Come on," he invited. "Don't applaud, just throw money."

"It's very ingenious, Gus," Malcolm acknowledged uncertainly. "But you've built up an entire murder plot from precious little. You could have got the whole thing totally round your neck."

"Possibly — you have another explanation?"

"But it's got gaps all over the place," Lucinda objected. "There are all sorts of questions you need answers to. How will you do that?"

"I met someone called Jack Bradshaw at a party about a year ago," he replied. "He's a former copper who now runs a private detective agency. I talked to him for quite a while and he seemed very good. I'll ring him in the morning."

"But he might come up with nothing at all," Tess objected. "You're just shooting in the dark with hardly anything to go on."

"And it won't hurt to try," Maltravers argued. "All right, I'm only guessing at the moment, but let's see if Bradshaw comes up with anything and take it from there."

"Gus, why don't you just tell the police all this?" Lucinda asked. "They could check it out much more easily than you can."

Maltravers shook his head firmly. "Not yet. I'm positive I could be on to something, but I'm not absolutely sure it's a murderer. There could be another explanation. If I do manage to find out enough to clinch it, I'll hand it all over to them. And if I don't manage to confirm anything, I'll have to forget it."

"This could take you some time," Malcolm remarked. "Are you sure it's safe to wait before telling the police? If you're right . . ."

"Another day or so won't matter," Maltravers said indifferently. "The murder's been done and the only one suffering at the moment is Lydden. From what I know about him, he deserves to sweat a bit."

In Carwelton Hall, Jennifer Carrington sat at her glass-topped dressing table, an engraved silver jewel box open in front of her. She picked up a ruby and emerald necklace which had belonged to Carrington's first wife, the facets of the stones hard and reassuring under her hand; she had never worn it. She needed the comfort of touching it, knowing its value and dependability, as the fact that things had gone wrong almost from the moment Charles had died kept coming back. It was no good being told not to worry as long as Duggie was still held by the police. Charlotte Quinn had come on Thursday afternoon — God alone knew why — which could ruin everything. Jennifer Carrington's fingers tightened round the necklace as she faced again the terrifying fact that she could be left alone and exposed, her lies torn to shreds, her guilt laid bare. But she could prove somebody else had lied as well.

The girl who answered the telephone next morning sounded bored and faintly irritated that she had been made to do some work.

"Bradshaw's Enquiry Agency."

"Is Mr Bradshaw there?" Maltravers asked.

"Yeah. Do you want to speak to him?"

"No. I'm just wasting time and money on a long distance phone call to check on his movements."

"You what?"

"Never mind, just put me through . . . hello? Gus Maltravers. We met at Laura Mazur's party in Lancaster Gate last year. Remember? That's right. I've got a job for you. If I give you the registration number of a car, can you find the name and address of the owner?"

"Unless the vehicle licensing centre at Swansea has gone on strike," Bradshaw replied. "It'll cost you though."

"I'm not worried about that. And once you've found it, I want some more information about the owner. How long would that take?"

"Depends how much you want to know. There are a lot of computers. I can give you his credit rating instantly, but if you're asking for his life history from his first measles jab to how much he's earning in his current job and what his mortgage is, it takes longer. Twenty-four hours to be on the safe side."

"That'll be fine, but don't bother with too much detail. All I really need to know is how long he's been at his present address, where he was before and what he does for a living."

"What's the car number?" Bradshaw sounded disappointed that the request was not more challenging.

"XCX 345X," Maltravers told him, "I don't know what make."

"That doesn't matter. Where can I get back to you? Got it. I'll call tomorrow morning."

Lucinda raised her eyebrows at Tess as Maltravers rang off.

"And this is the man who positively boasts of his ignorance about cars? How on earth did you remember that number?"

"Pure chance," he replied. "On long journeys I often pass the time by playing the old game of making up words from number plates. The rule is that the letters must occur in the same order, but not necessarily together. The XCX combination caught my eye because it was a tough one and you may remember me saying 'executrix' as we left Carwelton Hall the other night. The 345 and the final X were easy after that and . . ."

He was interrupted by the phone ringing. It was Malcolm with the news that Duggie Lydden was appearing in court that morning.

"They're charging him." Maltravers put the receiver down. "The evidence must all be circumstantial, but it's bloody strong and they daren't let him go. He's been very cleverly stitched up."

He looked at bright autumn sunshine biting through the living-room window, then turned to Tess. "Anyway, there's nothing I can do for the time being and it's a perfect day for a drive round the Lakes. There's a shop in Kendal I want to take you to as well."

Half an hour later, Charlotte Quinn was obsessed with restless, acid thoughts when the shop bell tinkled. She steeled herself to face another customer, somehow acting as though everything was normal, when she saw it was Maltravers with a woman she did not know.

"Hello, again," he said. "I promised I'd come back with Tess."

Charlotte smiled with relief. At least with him she would not have to clamp a total strait-jacket around her emotions.

"Of course you did. Are you interested in anything particular?"

"A good deal, I imagine," Tess replied, looking round the shop. "I think I can do half my Christmas shopping here."

She and Maltravers wandered round while Charlotte Quinn served other customers, but the shop was empty again as they went to pay for the things Tess had chosen.

"That's a hundred and fifty-four pounds thirty." Charlotte smiled thinly. "Call it a hundred and fifty."

"Discount on top of your prices?" Tess commented in surprise as she handed over her credit card. "I've already saved a small fortune. Do you know how much this sort of thing costs in London?"

"I could never charge that up here." Charlotte turned to Maltravers. "Anyway, I owe you a great deal. I don't know how I'd have coped on Thursday afternoon if you hadn't been there." Her face went bitter. "The pity is I didn't meet you before and have you tell me I should talk to Charles. If I'd found the courage to do that sooner, it might never have happened. That's what's so awful. I keep telling myself . . ."

"Then don't," Maltravers interrupted firmly. "You've nothing to blame yourself for."

"Yes there is," she contradicted savagely. "You don't know how much. Nobody does. Now it's something I've got to . . . do you know what I can't get out of my mind? What Sherlock Holmes says towards the end of Charles's book. 'Love destroys as often as it blesses.' You don't expect lines like that in detective stories."

While Charlotte Quinn had been talking, she had been absently playing with Tess's credit card in her hand; now she automatically reached for the machine to process it. Maltravers and Tess felt uncomfortable as they watched tears slipping down her face as she completed the sale and put Tess's purchases into green and gold Quintessence carrier bags. When she looked at them again, her eyes were empty and she seemed much older.

"It's been nice meeting you," she said to Tess. "I'm sorry I . . " She gestured helplessly, smearing her make-up as she rubbed a tear away.

"Don't apologise," Tess said gently. "Gus has told me about you and Charles. There's nothing adequate to say, is there?"

"No." Charlotte drew herself upright. "Thank you for not trying. People always feel they have to say something when they should just shut up. This is my problem and I'll deal with it my way. Goodbye."

As they walked away from Quintessence, Stricklandgate was full of the everyday bustle of the main street in a Lakeland market town. Traffic crawled noisily up the hill, people mingled on the pavements, a baby cried in a pram left outside a supermarket. Murder had inflicted drama, but they were all safely removed from its pain. Tess looked concerned as they made their way back to the car-park.

"That is one very unhappy woman," she said. "Why didn't you tell her what you think you could be on to?"

"For one thing, I could be wrong," Maltravers replied. "But there's more to it than that. When I first met Charlotte she was resentful, now she's bitter. If it turns out I am right, I certainly don't fancy telling her because then she's going to be very angry indeed."

They drove up to Keswick for lunch then went out of the town past Derwent Water into Borrowdale. Maltravers stopped in the shadow of the forbidding mass of Great Gable and they climbed its slopes until they could see the valley spread out before them, mottled greens and bracken browns, alternately lit and darkened by sunshine and scudding clouds. Tess lay back on short, tough, sheep-cropped grass beneath a crag of rock with Maltravers sitting beside her.

"What do you think Charlotte will do if you're right?" she asked.

"What would you do?"

Tess was silent for a moment. "First I'd weep. Then I'd wait until they released Jennifer Carrington. I wouldn't care how many years it was."

Maltravers twisted his head round and looked down at her. "And then?"

"Then I think I'd kill her."

"That would be a long time to carry hate."

"I'd have a lot of hatred to carry."

Late that afternoon, Charlotte Quinn stood in the drizzle outside a newsagents in Stricklandgate, reading the *Lancashire Evening Post* report of Lydden's court appearance by the light from the shop window. People milled about her, but she was oblivious of their existence. A placard reading 'Kendal Man on Murder Charge' stood by the doorway. She felt the numbed unreality that accompanies the experience of seeing something dreadful in a newspaper about someone you know. The *Post* had pushed the reporting restrictions of the Criminal Justice Act as far as it dared.

"Company director Douglas Keith Lydden, 44, appeared before Kendal magistrates today charged with the murder of Lancaster solicitor Charles Carrington.

Wearing a blue suit and open-necked shirt, the accused appeared in the dock between two police officers. No plea was entered, but when asked by chairman of the bench, Colonel Brian Harrison, if he had anything to say, Lydden replied in a clear voice: 'I did not do it.'

Lydden, of 27 Ruskin Close, Kendal, who owns an interior design shop in Stricklandgate, was further charged with the theft of ten books and a number of papers from Mr Carrington's home at Carwelton Hall, Attwater and with possession of a shotgun without a current firearms certificate.

An application for bail was refused and the accused was remanded in custody for seven days after Mr Michael Imeson, prosecuting, told the court that police enquiries were continuing. Committal proceedings to the Crown Court are expected to begin next week.

Mr Carrington, 61, was found dead at his home from gunshot wounds last Thursday. He had been in practice as a solicitor in

Lancaster for more than 30 years. His wife Jennifer was questioned by police after his death, but later released."

Accompanying the report was a picture of Charles Carrington taken from a larger group photograph at a Lancashire Law Society dinner the previous year. Charlotte Quinn remembered the original, with Charles happily standing next to a smiling Jennifer in the middle of a group in evening dress. Now some sub-editor had brutally cut him out of the picture, separating him from the rest as the dead were removed from the living. As she started to read the report again, as though to convince herself that it was true, a couple walked out of the shop behind her.

"Fancy that nice Mr Lydden being accused of murder!" the woman said. "We bought those curtains from him only a few weeks ago. Let's go and look at his shop. It's just down this way."

Charlotte Quinn quivered with fury as she watched them stop under the street lamp outside the closed door of Lakeland Interiors, peering through the darkened window. She wanted to run after them and physically shake them, screaming that 'nice Mr Lydden' was not fit to clean up vomit and had callously betrayed the man who had saved his business by jumping into bed with his tart of a wife. Let them think about that as they told their friends about who sold them their wretched and probably tasteless curtains. As the couple pointed in fascination at something in the window, glamourising pedestrian lives with someone else's tragedy, she almost started to go after them.

"Excuse me. Are you all right?"

Another man had come out of the newsagents and seen her, shuddering with emotion and face twisted with rage. She glared at him then ran back across the road to Quintessence. Her assistant looked up in alarm as she burst in, barging a customer aside as she rushed through and dashed upstairs to her flat. She slammed the door behind her and leaned against it, the newspaper crushed in her hand. She threw it down like something unclean as she clapped her hand to her retching mouth then ran into the bathroom and was sick.

Pale-faced, she returned to the living-room and poured a drink. As she sat recovering, swarming emotions began to overwhelm her. Not against Duggie Lydden; the courts would deal with him. It was the inescapable image of Jennifer Carrington that tortured her and boiled her anger. The woman who had wormed her way into the affections of a man she had then coldly cheated would now become the owner of Carwelton Hall. Charlotte Quinn's gnawing resentment began to consume her with unforgiving loathing.

She remained in the flat until her assistant came up and said she had closed for the night. Dismissing questions about what was the matter, Charlotte sent the girl home then went down into the shop. On one shelf was a collection of hunting knives. It was a line she had not wanted to stock, but there had been repeated requests from tourists and at least she had bought the best. The one she selected was Swiss, its end fashioned like the curve of a quarter moon to a needle-sharp point. She stared for a long time at the six inches of tempered steel, shining slightly with a smear of oil, scraping her thumb against the honed fineness of the blade's edge. The feeling that had been born when she saw Charles's body was now fully formed and possessed her. She thrust the knife back into its stitched leather sheath and took it upstairs.

Chapter Ten

Telephone wedged between chin and shoulder, Maltravers scribbled swift notes as he listened to Bradshaw on Tuesday morning.

"Geoffrey Martin Howard, aged thirty-five, address 307b Palatine Road, Didsbury, Manchester," he said. "Lived there for the past six years, immediate previous address his parents' home in Stockport, Cheshire. Civil engineering student at the University of Manchester, Institute of Science and Technology but dropped out half-way through the course. Went to Africa for a year — there's a smell of smuggling about that period — then came back. A couple of part-time jobs as a petrol station attendant and barman, but registered unemployed since 1983."

"Unemployed?" Maltravers queried. "He looked affluent enough when I met him."

"He would," Bradshaw said caustically. "Naughty boy, your Mr Howard, with a nice little earner. He doesn't need his dole money."

"What is it?"

"Drug pushing. But my mate in Criminal Records says he's too clever to be caught. He doesn't deal with the street junkies any more — too fly for that. He supplies the respectable middle classes who think it's all frightfully daring and a bit of fun. Stupid buggers."

"So he's got the sort of customers who can look after him if necessary," Maltravers remarked.

"You've got it," said Bradshaw. "They almost had him once but some high-powered city councillor — who's also a JP incidentally — put a stop to it with a few words in the right ears. Howard's been keeping him and his wife high for years. Anyway, that's the guts of it. I didn't bother with medical records or anything like that, but if you want . . ."

"No," Maltravers interrupted. "You've given me more than enough already. Send your bill to me in London. Thanks a lot."

He gave Bradshaw his home address then rang off and stood by the phone looking back through his notes. Tess tried to read them over his shoulder but his shorthand frustrated her.

"Well?" she asked.

"He's a clever liar. He used things that he's actually done to provide a cover story. And Bradshaw's just told me something else I didn't expect, which . . ." Maltravers idly corrected an outline, then turned to Lucinda. "When did Charles's daughter die?"

"Gillian? Five or six years ago."

"That's too vague. I need the year and the month and the date as well if possible. Who'd know?"

Lucinda looked unsure. "People who'd been friends of Charles's longer than us, but I don't know many of them. Except Charlotte of course. She'd certainly remember."

"I'd rather not ask her. What about Alan Morris, your vicar? He'd known Charles for years hadn't he?"

"Yes, and . . ." Lucinda stopped and gave a gesture of realisation. "You don't need to ask anybody. You can read it for yourself on the gravestone. Gillian's buried in Attwater churchyard."

"Buried? I thought all old village churchyards were full these days."

"There's a Carrington family plot going back to who knows when," Lucinda explained. "There's room for at least two more bodies in it."

"Whereabouts in the churchyard is it?" Maltravers asked.

"By the wall on the north side," Lucinda told him. "Right next to a monstrosity with weeping angels. You can't miss it. But how is it going to help you?"

"Because once I've got that date, Tess and I are going to Manchester to look something up," he replied. "I can't be sure it's going to work, but it's worth a try."

"You're still not going to tell the police?" Lucinda asked.

He shook his head. "Not yet. Lydden's been charged, which

must mean the police are fairly certain of their ground and a new theory from me, which is not absolutely complete, is hardly likely to fill them with joy. They'll have to investigate, but official procedures could take time. By this afternoon I could have tied up the loose ends and can hand the whole thing over to them."

"But aren't you withholding evidence or something?" Lucinda argued.

"If I am, it's still shaky evidence," he replied. "By the end of the day, it could be definite. A few enquiries in Manchester will sort it out and nothing's lost in the meantime. Nobody's going to run away while the police still have those books."

In his office at Kendal police station, Lambert looked discontented as his slouched figure overflowed the sides of his chair.

"I know Lydden's type," he told Moore. "Guilty as Old Harry, but screams his innocence in the hope that some sharp defence counsel will get him off on a technicality."

"His lawyer keeps protesting it's circumstantial, sir."

Lambert grunted. "They only had circumstantial evidence that Nixon knew about Watergate. Anyway, we've got at least to give the impression that we think it still could be someone else, though God knows who it could be. How's it going?"

"The lads are checking on the names and addresses of all Charles Carrington's known friends and associates which we drew up from his private address book, his secretary and his wife. They've been told to pay particular attention to anyone who says they've read this Sherlock Holmes book. I can't see anything else we can do."

"Bloody waste of time. The sooner we can drop this and get more men on that rape enquiry in Penrith the better."

Detective Constable Ian Drover was one of six officers assigned to further enquiries among Charles Carrington's friends. As he drove to the first address, his mind constantly returned to his interview with the Reverend Morris. That morning he had almost asked Moore if he could speak to him and explain that . . . Drover shook his head in rejection. It was unthinkable. Among his earliest childhood memories was having tea at the vicarage and when his mother had been ill, Mr Morris had called in almost every day. It didn't matter that . . . Drover reached his destination and pushed his worries to the back of his mind, but they haunted him throughout the rest of the day.

Eternally piled in strata of coffins, six generations of Carringtons lay in the double plot beneath a wind-blasted blackthorn tree against the granite wall of the little Attwater churchyard. Somewhere at the bottom was Emily Faith, who died in childbirth the year of the Great Exhibition; near the top lay Gillian Zoe, dead from another agony more than a century later. The column of corpses was a mute record of social change, the very names changing with the lifestyles. Immediately above Gillian's name was that of her brother David which followed their mother. The grave was well tended, and Maltravers felt that Carrington had almost certainly paid some villager to keep it in order. It would have been an agony for him to have come to the spot which contained the bodies of so many he had loved, memories of vibrant lives shared made intolerable by carved records of tragic deaths.

"Gillian died on her birthday," he commented as he and Tess looked at the gravestone. "She would have been twenty-four — which means she was actually older than Jennifer."

"And presumably Charles will be buried here as well." Tess shivered. "God this is depressing. Let's get away from here."

As they walked back to where Maltravers had parked in the lane, Alan Morris watched them from the front room of the vicarage. He recognised Maltravers, but Tess was a stranger and he wondered why they had been taking an interest in that particular grave.

"Where first?" Tess asked as Maltravers drove down the sliproad on to the southbound carriageway of the M6.

"Deansgate," he replied. "The *Evening News* offices to see what we can find there, then Sherratt & Hughes."

It took less than an hour and a half to reach the city centre and Maltravers parked in the multi-storey near the Crown Court building. They walked past the old northern offices of the *Daily Mail*, now closed since the computer age and the accountants had moved all production to London, and into the *Manchester Evening News* where Maltravers asked to see Peter Harris, a colleague from his own earliest reporting days, now the paper's Medical Correspondent. Having a contact short-circuited the system and they were taken straight to the editorial library where an assistant loaded the viewer for them with the microfilms for July and August 1984.

"She died on the twenty-second of July and the inquest should have been during the next few weeks," Maltravers said as he wound the handle and the pages flickered across the screen. "Keep your eyes peeled."

He only had to check through one edition to work out the editorial pattern, skipping past the national and foreign news, sport and feature pages and concentrating on the northern news sections. The first reference was a single paragraph stating that an inquest on Gillian Carrington had been opened and adjourned, then they found the full report three weeks later. Maltravers instinctively glanced at the final sentence; verdicts invariably appeared at the end.

"Death by misadventure," he said, then went back to the beginning as Tess reached forward and pointed half-way down the column.

"There he is." For a few moments they read in silence.

"Same address Bradshaw gave me," Maltravers commented. "Described himself as an unemployed barman and last saw Gillian two weeks before they found her body. He knew she'd been an addict for some years."

"That's it then," Tess said.

"Just about," Maltravers agreed. "Let's check Sherratt & Hughes."

The shop was crowded when they walked in and Maltravers watched the transactions at the cash desk as they both idly flicked through books they took from the shelves. He selected the new Mary Wesley and went to pay for it with his credit card.

"What do you think?" Tess asked as they left.

"It's only negative proof, of course," he replied. "But that's all I expected. If we can confirm the link, that's it."

"Which means my little starring role," said Tess. "Let's have lunch somewhere first."

They drove out of the city centre to a restaurant in Didsbury which Maltravers remembered from his time in Manchester. After they had eaten, Tess went to the ladies room and Maltravers smiled appreciatively as she reappeared. She had wound her hair up in a bun style she never wore and her features had been flattened by skilfully applied make-up. She spoke to the waiter as she crossed the room and her natural London voice had totally changed, not to obvious broad northern but to the accent of the Cheshire county set, vowels subtly widened, the 'G' at the end of the present participles faintly audible.

"The rehearsal went well," Maltravers remarked, nodding at the waiter as she sat down again. "He's trying to work out why I'm having lunch with two different women."

"So you don't think anybody will recognise me?" Tess asked.

"Darling, *I* don't recognise you," he replied. "Come on, let's get to Palatine Road."

As Maltravers had expected from the address, the detached house in the suburbs was a typical home of an Industrial Revolution businessman, originally big enough to accommodate an entire Victorian family and servants, now converted, like its neighbours, into flats. The garden at the front had been concreted over to provide car-parking, but the rest of the property was well preserved with new maroon paint on the woodwork and the front door's flower pattern of leaded stained-glass intact.

"Upmarket flats," he commented as they looked at the house from the opposite side of the road. "Too many of these places haven't been looked after properly. All right, know your lines?"

"Naturally," Tess replied. "I'm looking up an old friend called Jennifer Davenport and this is the last address I've got for her. When he says he's never heard of her, I ask if he knows of anyone called Jennifer who's lived here because she might have got married and have a different surname. After that, I hope for the best."

"Not a plan with any guarantee of success, but he might let something slip out and it's worth trying as long as we're here," said Maltravers. "I'll wait round the corner past those traffic lights. I don't want to risk him seeing me. Good luck."

Tess got out and heard Maltravers drive away as she crossed the road and walked up to the house. There were five bells set in a two-way intercom next to the front door and she pressed the one with Howard's name beside it on a strip of card. There was no reply. She tried twice more without success then examined the rest of the names. One of the cards looked much older than the rest and when she pressed the button a voice echoed out of the loudspeaker.

"Who is it?" Distorted and tinny, the voice still sounded friendly. Tess leaned forward.

"I'm sorry to trouble you, but . . ."

More than an hour and a half later, an increasingly anxious Maltravers saw her appear round the corner. He reached across and let the passenger door swing open as she approached.

"You are aware that soliciting is an offence are you, sir?" She looked stern as she bent down and peered at him. "I am a plainclothes police officer and . . ."

"Stop clowning about. I was getting worried."

Tess climbed in beside him and he looked at her enquiringly.

"I've been talking to a retired headmistress called Miss Ashton," she explained. "She's eighty-three years old and has a Pekinese called Loo-Che, smokes Capstan Full Strength, would you believe, and serves Bath Olivers and Earl Grey to complete strangers. She's marvellous."

"Fascinating," said Maltravers caustically. "I'm delighted you enjoyed yourself. Did you happen to find anything out as well?"

"Oh, yes," Tess told him with affected casualness. "She knows that Geoffrey Howard has gone to London for a few days because he asked her to keep his post for him . . . and she remembers his girlfriend very well. But she doesn't think she was called Jennifer Davenport. Something like Boyd, she thinks it was."

"Lloyd," said Maltravers triumphantly. "We've cracked it. But what's he gone to London for?"

"According to Miss Ashton, he often goes there on business. He's connected with Far Eastern imports in some way."

"Imports of white powder in plastic bags." Maltravers glanced at Tess. "Do you think your Miss Ashton realises that?"

"No," Tess said firmly. "She thinks he's a very charming young man. I quote. He must put up a good act."

"He does," Maltravers confirmed. "I've seen it."

Tess leaned across and kissed him on the cheek. "All right, who's a clever boy then? Now stop looking so damned smug. Let's go back and tell it all to the police and they can give you a putty medal."

"I think we might make one final call before that," he replied. "Just for the fun of it."

Tess glanced at him sharply. "What are you talking about?"

"I'll tell you on the way back."

As Maltravers drove over the soaring motorway bridge crossing the Manchester Ship Canal, they heard a radio traffic report that a lorry had shed its load south of Preston and there were already long tailbacks building up ahead of them. They wound through coils of overlapping roads spun round the edges of the city before joining an endless line of traffic which crawled with agonising slowness before everything stopped; the radio announced that queues were now stretching back for six miles and drivers should try alternative routes. Maltravers swore.

"We'll go off at the next exit, assuming we ever reach it," he said. "It'll be slower through the towns, but at least we'll keep moving."

"How long will it take?" Tess asked.

Maltravers stepped out of the car and peered as far as he could along the stationary vehicles ahead of them. He glanced at his watch as he got back in.

"We should make it by about eight o'clock with a bit of luck," he said. "Good job there's no panic."

Standing rigidly to attention, Ian Drover was petrified as Lambert slouched behind his desk like a brooding Buddha, silently considering everything he had now been told about the interview with Alan Morris. Next to his chief, Donald Moore looked grim.

"One whole hour from three thirty he won't tell us about?" Lambert repeated. He sounded like someone who had just learned that Margaret Thatcher had turned up after a secret flight to Moscow and confessed to having been a lifelong agent for the KGB. "Says it was confidential? And you accepted it?"

"It was a private matter involving one of his parishioners," Drover explained. He was too nervous to see that Lambert's apparent calm was on a hair trigger. "He told me he gave his word that he would never divulge anything about it to anyone, sir."

Lambert looked at the young constable as though he could not believe he existed. "Somebody come down with AIDS have they? Or is the Reverend Morris having his end away with the verger's wife? Or one of the bloody choirboys?" His voice exposed the edge of anger as it emerged out of his incredulity that any CID officer could be so naive and disobedient.

"Mr Morris is . . ." Drover looked helplessly at Moore for support but the sergeant stared back icily. "You're not local, sir. Anyone will tell you what sort of a man he is. He'd never do anything that . . . he's a member of the Rotary Club!"

"I don't care if he's on first name terms with the Princess of bloody Wales!" Lambert bellowed. "He's got a bleeding great gap in his movements at the time of the murder! And you let him get away with trying to bring the sanctity of the confessional into it! Why the hell didn't you report this before?"

Lambert glowered like a raging bull regathering strength for another charge as Drover looked down at his shoes.

"I didn't think it was important," he mumbled.

"You didn't think it was important." Lambert let every word drop separately, like bricks on a tin tray. Drover flinched and stepped back as the superintendent stood up like the wrath of God. For a moment he thought his boss was going to physically assault him.

"There is a man in the nick the police have brought charges against and now I find there could be another suspect." Lambert's voice was a fuse hissing towards dynamite. "But because Mr Morris used to pat you on the head after church when you were a kid, you decided he has to be innocent. You've deliberately ignored evidence because you don't want to believe it. How the hell did they let you into the CID, Drover?" A very short pause followed the question, then the dynamite exploded. "Because you're not bloody well staying there! You're suspended! And if they ever let you back, you'll be lucky if they put you in charge of a fucking school-crossing patrol on a Sunday! Now get out of here!"

The shattered detective constable looked as though he had been hit by a falling house as he instinctively saluted in nervous terror and left. The door closed and Lambert crashed back into his chair, putting his head in his hands.

"Why did you send him to see Morris?" he asked bleakly.

"I'm sorry, sir." Moore looked uncomfortable. "He volunteered and I thought a local man might be best. He's fairly new to the CID, but he's got a good record and I never thought that . . ."

"Then think next time," Lambert's face appeared wearily from behind the great hams of his hands. "Never send a villager to the village. And if that little prat's religious beliefs have landed us in it, then St Michael and all his bloody angels won't be able to save him from me."

"But what sort of motive is there for Morris?" Moore argued. "He'd known Carrington for years and it can't have been money because . . ."

"They pay us to find out things like that, sergeant," Lambert interrupted. "And even the Archbishop of Canterbury doesn't get away with lines like Morris is using. See him again — and you go this time. Either he comes up with a full explanation of what he was up to for that hour or he'll have to come here and have a little chat with me. I want you back here in an hour, either with him or a satisfactory story."

As Moore was leaving the office, Lambert spoke again.

"I still think it's Lydden," he said. "And I don't want to have made a mistake and have him able to come up with a charge of wrongful arrest."

In Stricklandgate, Charlotte Quinn sat in her flat, slowly turning the pages of a photograph album on the table in front of her. The hunting knife lay alongside a bell-bottomed ship's decanter from which she steadily drank neat vodka. There were pictures of herself and her family on holiday with the Carringtons in the Algarve fifteen years earlier; the children in the swimming pool; herself and her husband on the beach with Margaret; Charles laughing at the camera as he was caught off guard eating a watermelon on the patio of the villa. Six of those people in the pictures, all of whom she had loved in different ways, were now dead while Jennifer Carrington was still alive, young, happy and about to become very rich. She would be as indifferent to her lover being jailed for life as she was to him having murdered her own husband; Lydden had been a meaningless sex object and she had never been a wife in any sense Charlotte Quinn could accept.

She slammed the album shut as bitter memories and coruscating resentment became unbearable. Wracked by all-consuming, disorientating hatred, she moaned and bent forward, hands clutched to her abdomen.

"Charles," she whispered. "Oh my darling, darling Charles."

She raised weeping eyes to where the unsheathed blade of the hunting knife shone like a sacrificial dagger on the altar of demanding gods.

Chapter Eleven

"Reverend . . . Morris." Lambert's voice dropped an octave between the title and the surname as he examined Moore's report without looking up. "When I was at school, they taught us about something called benefit of clergy. Very useful it was. If you could read, they didn't hang you."

Lambert raised his enquiring, bullfrog of a face, the ball-bearing eyes piercing like lasers.

"However, I happen to remember my teacher telling me it was abolished in 1827, so it doesn't concern us. What were you doing between half past three and half past four last Thursday afternoon?"

"I have already explained to your sergeant that I can see no reason to tell you, superintendent." Morris returned Lambert's stare without flinching. "You have my assurance that it was not connected with the murder of Charles Carrington. That ought to be sufficient."

Lambert leaned across the desk, his fingers interlocking.

"It would be for some. It satisfied DC Drover." Morris looked away. "But, you see, I'm a Methodist. Now we've got a number of options. I could arrest you on suspicion and haul you up before a magistrate. We could call your solicitor so that he can explain the law to you. I could waste time making enquiries in Attwater . . . or you could tell me." Lambert smiled. "Let's go for that."

Morris sighed and closed his eyes. He had had nightmares about this moment.

Lowry's industrial Lancashire of smoking mills, corner tripe shops and cramped back-to-back terraces where the front room was kept 'for best' or ham sandwich funerals had almost disappeared. As they drove through the old cotton towns, Maltravers found the functional tower blocks and endless anonymous estates with a token presence of trees and the mustard glare of street lights on concrete posts in many ways more depressing than what they had replaced. The indigenous echoes of George Formby's ukelele and Gracie Fields's soprano had faded completely, swamped by electronic disco music in dazzling multicoloured neon caverns, indistinguishable from a thousand other towns. A gritty north country individuality had been lost in carbon copy modern shopping centres with homogenous supermarkets and bleak new pubs where Muzak seeped out of flocked wallpaper. There had been a harsh, tough romance about wooden clogs clattering along cobbled back alleys and tin baths in front of the black lead grate in the kitchen; however grim it had been, it had at least had a personality. Now there was hot and cold water from cheap chromium taps, colour television and the mill girls's granddaughters played bingo in Majorca.

"Charles Carrington's last journey," he remarked as they rejoined the M6 beyond Lancaster. "Of course, nobody was supposed to find the body until Jennifer got home in the evening, but Charlotte must have arrived minutes after it happened. They must have been worrying about that. The idea was that Duggie Lydden would have needed an alibi to cover several hours, which can be almost impossible. Having the murder pinned down to within half an hour or so was very different."

"But he still can't have had one."

"Obviously not, but murder plans that go adrift right from the start don't make for peace of mind."

"Are you sure about what you're doing when we get back?" Tess asked uncertainly. "You've got everything you need to go to the police."

"Of course I'm going to the police," he said. "Eventually. But after all I've done, I think I deserve the satisfaction of trying to dig out a confession myself first. There's no risk. Trust me."

There were lights showing as they passed Carwelton Hall and Jennifer Carrington's car was in the drive.

"Malcolm and Lucinda will have been wondering how we've gone on, so we'll tell them first then come back," Maltravers said. "After that the police can have the whole lot with my compliments."

Malcolm had just returned from working late at the office and he and Lucinda listened in fascination as Maltravers explained how he and Tess had confirmed the final pieces of the story.

"This is going to be one hell of a court case." Malcolm shook his head in disbelief as Maltravers finished. "Would you write a backup piece for the *Chronicle* when it's over?"

"I think I'd like to do that," Maltravers agreed. "And I may be able to make it an even better read with one last thing. Jennifer is still at Carwelton Hall and I'm going to see her."

"What?" Malcolm sounded alarmed. "You're not going to face her with it are you?"

"Of course not, the police can do that," Maltravers assured him, straight-faced. "But it would be interesting to see if an idle chat reveals anything to fill in the odd corner."

"But what's your excuse?" Malcolm argued. "She'll be suspicious if you just turn up for no reason."

"I've got the perfect reason. I promised Charles Carrington I would return *The Attwater Firewitch* and I'm giving it back to his widow. It's presumably her property now. Tess can come with me and we'll see what happens . . . if anything."

Maltravers parked on the road beyond the bend outside Carwelton Hall half an hour later.

"There's no point in taking the car in, we won't be staying long," he remarked as they walked back.

"For the last time, I think you're mad," Tess said warningly as he opened the gate and they stepped on to the drive. Ahead of them, several downstairs lights were on and there was a glow from behind the curtains at a bedroom window. "We should be going straight to the police. Your taste for the theatrical will get you into trouble one day."

"But not this evening," he said confidently. "Howard's in London, probably collecting another consignment of drugs, while

Jennifer waits for Duggie Lydden to be sentenced then they take off with the loot. I think I've earned tonight's little indulgence."

Jennifer Carrington looked nervous as she opened the front door, then invited them in and took them through to the sitting-room.

"We're going back to London at the weekend," Maltravers added after he had introduced Tess. "I wasn't sure how long you'd be here, so I thought I'd better return this to you while I had the chance. I promised Charles I'd bring it back."

"Oh, of course. I'd forgotten you had it," Jennifer Carrington took the envelope containing the Conan Doyle photocopy. "The police still have the books, but my solicitor says I should get them back soon . . . would you like a drink?"

"Thank you." Maltravers watched as she walked across to the drinks cabinet. "One of Malcolm's reporters has heard that Duggie Lydden's shotgun has been found. Did you know?"

Jennifer Carrington paused fractionally, but did not turn round. "No. Where was it?"

"Hidden somewhere near his house apparently. The fact that they've charged him suggests they must have proved it was the murder weapon . . ." Maltravers shrugged. "Perhaps he'll tell the truth eventually."

"I hope so." She poured the drinks and handed them their glasses. "I never knew anyone could hate as much as he does. He seems determined to mix me up in it somehow."

"What are you going to do?" Tess asked. "When it's all over. Will you stay here?"

"I don't know at the moment. I've got a lot of good memories in this house, but . . ." she gestured helplessly. "I'll have to think about it."

"I was wondering if you might go back to Manchester," Maltravers said. "You must have friends there."

"Not many . . . and nobody special." Jennifer Carrington turned away to put her glass down as she replied. "I might leave England altogether and try to start again."

She appeared guarded as they talked casually for another few minutes, then Maltravers finished his drink and stood up.

"We must go," he said. "We just came to return the manuscript while you were here and say goodbye." He held out his hand. "I haven't had the chance to tell you how sorry I am about what's happened. I hardly knew Charles, but I liked him."

Jennifer Carrington lowered her head as she took his hand, touching only the ends of his fingers.

"He was a wonderful man," she said softly. "I loved him very much."

"Could I ask one thing before we leave?" Tess said. "Gus has told me about how he worked out the combination for the safe. May I see it?" She looked hesitant. "No, I'm sorry. It will upset you and . . ."

"It's all right," Jennifer Carrington interrupted. "I'm very grateful to him for that. It's something I couldn't have known. Come on through."

They followed her across the hall and into the library where Maltravers demonstrated how the figures from the Sherlock Holmes story unfastened the lock. But this time it did not work.

"I must have got one of the numbers wrong," he said. "Could you get the manuscript? You left it on the table in the other room. As long as I open this quickly enough, the alarm won't go off."

As Jennifer Carrington walked out, he rapidly spun the dial and opened the safe, putting something from his pocket on the shelf before relocking the door. When she came back, he went through the pantomime of consulting the manuscript and repeating the operation.

"Quod erat demonstrandum," he said to Tess, opening the door again. "Which means that Duggie Lydden must have read . . . hello, what's this?"

He reached inside the safe and took out the envelope he had placed there moments before, turning to Jennifer Carrington quizzically.

"Surely the police would have noticed this," he said. "Or did you put it there yourself afterwards? It has your name on."

"What? But it was empty when . . . let me see that."

She snatched the envelope from him and tore it open then read the single sheet of paper inside.

"What does it say?" Maltravers asked quietly.

"'It has long been an axiom of mine that the little things are infinitely the most important'." Jennifer Carrington stared at him in bewilderment. "What does it mean? How did it get there?"

"I put it there," he said. "The quotation is from Conan Doyle, who keeps cropping up."

There was sudden alarm in Jennifer Carrington's face.

"What are you talking about?" she demanded.

"Murder of course," Maltravers replied quietly. "And a very clever murder at that. Whose idea was it in the first place?"

"What do you mean, whose idea?" Jennifer Carrington's alarm was deepening to panic. "You know that Duggie killed Charles. For God's sake you helped to prove it."

"Yes, I did, didn't I?" he agreed. "With my brilliant discovery about this safe combination. That was one of the things you were counting on wasn't it? If I hadn't done it, you'd have had to find another way to bring it out. However, I've now seen my mistake."

Jennifer Carrington controlled herself with a visible effort.

"Look, I don't know what you think you're doing. But I've been through more than enough the past few days with people being unkind to me without sick jokes. Now just get out of here and leave me alone. Both of you."

She stalked to the library door and stood next to it, implicitly ordering them out. Neither of them moved.

"It's no good, Jennifer," Maltravers told her. "We know that Duggie Lydden didn't kill Charles . . . and we also know who did."

For a moment she stared at him coldly then turned to Tess.

"Will you make him leave?"

"There's no point," Tess told her. "We know an awful lot."

"Even that it all started a long time ago when Geoffrey Howard met Gillian Carrington," Maltravers added.

Jennifer Carrington's eyes flashed back to him in horror then her face flared with anger.

"You're mad!" she shouted. "Now just get out!"

Maltravers glanced at Tess then picked up the telephone on the desk beside him. "We're wasting our time. I'll ring the police from here." As he lifted the receiver, Jennifer Carrington screamed.

"Geoffrey!"

The sound of footsteps racing down the stairs mixed with the clatter of Maltravers dropping the instrument.

"I thought you said he was in London!"

He pushed Jennifer Carrington roughly to one side as he leapt across to the doorway and tried to slam it closed but it flew open, sending him staggering backwards as Howard burst in. Jennifer Carrington ran to his side, throwing her arms round him. Seeing what he was holding, Maltravers moved to stand by Tess.

"What's going on?" Howard demanded.

"We were just having a little chat about murder," Maltravers replied with as much calmness as he could manage. "I wish I'd known you were here or I'd have been more careful."

"What's he talking about?" Howard asked Jennifer.

"He's guessed something somehow." She sobbed in terror. "He was just going to call the police."

"For God's sake, I warned you we shouldn't have come here," Tess murmured. "That thing looks real."

Standing next to the slight figure of Jennifer Carrington exaggerated Howard's formidable build and the menace was heightened by the revolver in his hand. Maltravers had never been threatened with a gun before — he could not even remember ever having seen one — and he found that the blue-black end of the barrel carried a hypnotic fascination. Simply going straight to the police would have been considerably safer and more sensible. Geoffrey Howard and Jennifer Carrington had already committed one carefully planned and premeditated murder and were now in an isolated house with no witnesses, where they could kill again and run. If it had not been so terrifyingly real, it would have been a farcical recreation of a moth-eaten cliché.

"How much do you know?" Howard asked him.

"Enough." Maltravers's mind raced as he indicated the revolver. "And that won't help you. I've told Malcolm and Lucinda Stapleton and they know we've come here tonight. If the police find two more bodies in this house you won't be able to explain them away."

He waited anxiously, reflecting that it sounded like another ancient formula, as Howard remained silent. It could be an hour or more before Malcolm and Lucinda became concerned. He stiffened as Howard worked that out for himself.

"We won't be here." He turned to Jennifer Carrington. "Go and pack and we'll catch a night flight from Manchester. We'll be miles away before they find these two. Hurry up."

"And leave the books behind?" Maltravers was frantically grasping at any argument he could think of. "That was the point of all this."

"Of course it was." Howard shrugged. "But we can't do anything about that now can we? We'll settle for the jewellery. That's worth enough."

Maltravers felt Tess take hold of his hand and squeeze it very hard; he realised that their palms were sweating. As he tried to think, his mind was insanely screaming that both of them were within minutes of death. He was obsessed with the thought that the situation was the result of his own conceit and he had only himself to blame; but Tess, who had tried to warn him, would die as well, which was intolerable.

"Think a minute," he said urgently. "You planned Charles's murder and you can still get away with it — we're in no position to stop you now. But do you really want to risk two more murders? You could lock us up somewhere in this place and still give yourselves time to get away."

Howard looked at him for what seemed a very long time, then turned to Jennifer Carrington. "Is there anywhere?"

"They wouldn't be able to get out of the cellar," she said. "And we could tie them up."

Had Maltravers been more detached, he would have had time to be fascinated that in such circumstances the mind of an agnostic could farcically throw up the name of St Barbara, patron saint of those in danger of sudden death. Waiting for Howard to decide, he put it down to some form of internal hysteria, but slipped in some sort of jumbled prayer.

"All right," Howard said finally then turned to Jennifer Carrington. "But we'll make absolutely sure. Get my stuff from upstairs."

"What stuff?" Maltravers, who had felt a swarm of relief as Howard had agreed, had a sick feeling that he knew.

"Heroin. Not enough to kill you, but you'll be in no state to talk to anybody for a long time. Don't worry." Howard smiled sourly. "I know what I'm doing. You'll be all right — eventually."

"Oh, Christ," Tess whispered.

Maltravers had a hideous image of Howard holding the revolver against Tess's head as Jennifer Carrington made the first injection into his own arm. What it would be like after that was impossible to conceive but, faced with the threat of death, he discovered that you leapt at anything that offered survival. He was desperately trying to think of some argument to change Howard's mind when the front doorbell rang.

"Don't answer it," Howard told Jennifer Carrington sharply. "They'll go away."

"I doubt it," Maltravers put in hastily. "Her car's in the drive and there are lights on all over the place."

"They'll go away," Howard repeated confidently.

At least it bought them time; Howard would surely not shoot while there was someone outside who might hear. As they waited in silence, Maltravers moved slightly so that Tess was on his left. If he could push her to one side then dive at Howard's feet, perhaps the bullet would go wide and he could . . . Howard gestured slightly with the gun, indicating they should move apart and stepped back, leaving an impossible distance between himself and Maltravers. The bell rang again.

"Are you expecting anyone?" Howard asked quietly. Jennifer Carrington shook her head. "All right, they'll get fed up eventually."

Maltravers began to wonder how calm Howard really was. The hand holding the gun had twitched fractionally at the second ring of the bell. Would whoever it was outside hear if he shouted loudly enough? It would almost certainly mean Howard would shoot him, but in the panic that would follow Tess might somehow escape. Permutations of possible results rattled through his mind. Would Howard shoot Tess immediately then rush out to deal with the visitor in the same way? Or would he dash straight to the front door first? Howard raised the revolver and held it towards them, extended hands clasped rigidly in front of him. Suddenly he seemed chillingly controlled.

Silence stretched through the room then it was broken by the bell again, but this time it rang endlessly. The shrill single note drilled on and on, seeming to grow louder and more insistent as it filled every corner of the house. After half a minute, Howard became agitated.

"For fuck's sake get rid of them!" he snapped. "Go on!"

Jennifer Carrington left the library and closed the door. The bell kept ringing. Howard mouthed the words 'keep quiet' at Maltravers then swung the gun in a slight arc towards Tess. He would shoot her first. In the hall the relentless noise abruptly stopped and there was an echoing quiet. They heard voices but the words were muffled, then a woman shouted and there was the sound of something falling as Jennifer Carrington screamed Howard's name again.

Maltravers tensed as Howard jerked his head round, keeping the gun raised. Almost immediately there was another shriek, this time of pain. Howard grabbed hold of the door and opened it; Jennifer Carrington was on the floor of the hall, struggling to free herself from another figure. Howard hesitated for a second then dashed towards them and Maltravers leapt through the library door after him, hurling one leg forwards to trip him up. He was half aware of the gun clattering across the parquet floor and Tess racing past as he clawed at Howard, then he was desperately trying to grab hold of the man when there was a thundering explosion and huge shards of clattering glass cascaded down from the frame of a portrait on one wall. A bullet hole piercing his neck, Sir Francis Carrington, JP stared impassively at the tableau of shocked and paralysed figures. Maltravers scrambled to his feet and ran over to Tess.

"Noisy but effective," he grasped, glancing up at the portrait as he took the revolver from her limp and shaking hand. "Good shot."

"Don't be stupid!" Her voice was trembling. "The bloody thing just went off!"

Maltravers whirled round and pointed the gun at Howard as he heard him start to move.

"I haven't much idea about how these things work, but at this range the odds are against you," he warned, fervently hoping Howard would not call his bluff. If he had to shoot, he could end up hitting anything or anybody, including himself. "Tess, call the police and we'll need an ambulance as well."

As Tess went back into the library, Maltravers crossed to Charlotte Quinn, lying dazed just inside the front door. He stooped and removed the hunting knife from limp fingers. Jennifer Carrington groaned on the floor next to her, clasped hands trying to staunch the blood flowing from her thigh. Watching Howard carefully, Maltravers helped Charlotte to a chair. She glared at him resentfully.

"Why didn't you let me kill her? She's going to have everything."

"No she's not," he promised. "She'll never get Carwelton Hall or anything in it."

Howard had moved next to Jennifer, cradling her head in one arm, vivid crimson spreading through the handkerchief he was holding against her wound. Tess came back into the hall.

"See if you can find some bandages," Maltravers told her. "Try in the bathroom." Howard looked up at him with loathing as Tess went upstairs.

"All right, you clever bastard. How did you get on to us?"

"Just two little mistakes," Maltravers told him. "And you made both of them. Sherlock Holmes helped me see them."

"I'm not in the mood for jokes," Howard snapped.

"None of us is," said Maltravers feelingly. "However, I'm not joking. It happened after dinner the other evening, although I didn't spot anything at the time. When you walked in front of me through that library door, you didn't bang your head like I did, and you're taller than I am. How did you know you had to duck if you hadn't been here before? Charles can't have warned you or he'd have called the same thing to me. Then, as you were leaving, you went left out of the gates instead of right towards the motorway. You can learn a lot during ten years in Nigeria, but not the safest way to turn out of Carwelton Hall because of the bend.

"The door was like the dog in Conan Doyle's story *Silver Blaze*, where Holmes makes the famous observation that it failed to bark in the night — something that should have happened but didn't. When you left, you did it in reverse. Something you shouldn't have done, you did."

Tess came downstairs with a roll of bandages and gave it to Howard who tore open Jennifer Carrington's skirt from the gash the knife had made and began to wind the material round the cut. She had fainted. Tess crossed the hall and put her arm around Charlotte Quinn. Howard ripped the end of the bandage apart and tied it before raising his face to Maltravers defiantly.

"Is that all you've got?" he asked scornfully. "Accusing me of murder because I didn't bang my head and how I drove out of the gate? You're out of your mind."

"Believe that if you want," Maltravers replied indifferently. "You'll find out how much more I know eventually. In the meantime you'd better start thinking up an explanation both for threatening to kill us just now and that heroin you've got upstairs."

He turned to Charlotte Quinn. "You shouldn't have come here tonight. Would it have made things any better?"

"It would for her," Tess told him sharply. "I've done the wrong thing for the right reasons before now. Anyway, she saved our lives. We shouldn't have come either."

"I know," Maltravers agreed. "But Howard might have killed her if we hadn't done."

Chapter Twelve

Alan Morris had discovered that, planted in forgotten childhood, some deep-rooted personal belief in what constituted sin denied him the final shield of untruth. Whatever else he could do, he was finally unable to lie. Lambert's professional instincts had recognised the weakness and relentlessly exploited it, cutting off each avenue of prevarication and escape until defeat was wearily accepted. As the whole story poured out with increasing willingness and a perverse sense of relief, the room had turned into a confessional.

Once the barriers were breached, Morris appeared compelled to confess everything. Eyes glittering with increasing excitement, he began with the four horses backed in an accumulator bet on the afternoon of the murder, the winnings from one passing on to the next. First a winner at 100–8, then another at evens, followed by a terrifyingly close 15–4 by half a length. Then the 20–1 outsider, agonisingly trailing in fifth as Morris had listened to the commentary in a betting shop. Five thousand desperate pounds, multiplying with ecstatic promise of deliverance until it vanished in the mud of Doncaster. The all-consuming thrill had possessed Morris again as he talked, the compulsion to retaste the intoxication of what might have been growing irresistible. For another hour he went back over years secretly filled with alternate elation of victory and growing despair of loss. He had stopped abruptly, staring at Lambert in disbelief as though unable to grasp what had happened. It had taken the suspicion of being a murderer to drive him to admit that he was a compulsive gambler, that the respectable, correct vicar was the helpless victim of a terrible sickness. His façade had crumbled and Lambert was left facing a bewildered man stripped of his reputation, withered by his weakness. The vicar had looked at his confessor in supplication, but there could be no absolution.

"Whose money was it, Mr Morris?"

There was a very long silence.

"I think I would like to make a statement."

With its immediate comprehension of the situation, Lambert's quietly-spoken question had torn away the last shreds of Alan Morris's spurious self-delusion; the tired reply had acknowledged his own destruction.

He had been released with a warning that there would be further police enquiries and Lambert's incredulity had been mixed with an overwhelming relief that Duggie Lydden was still his man. As he learned about the events at Carwelton Hall, he began to rumble like a volcano. Jennifer Carrington had been taken to hospital where the police were waiting until she could be questioned. The others were giving their statements and the spectre of wrongful arrest reappeared.

"That bugger again?" he exploded when he heard Maltravers's name. "First he tells us about seeing Lydden's car and then comes up with the story of the safe combination. Now this. Is he a private detective or something?"

"No, sir. He's a writer," Moore told him.

"What of? Bloody fairy-tales?" Lambert's giant goblin features, never attractive, twisted into hideous fury. "Where is he?"

He rolled tank-like through the corridors to the interview room where Maltravers had just completed his statement. The gargantuan detective picked it up and read it for himself then looked at him with distaste.

"You've been putting yourself about a bit haven't you?" he said. "How did you find all this out?"

"Inspiration, guesswork and luck," Maltravers replied. "Some of the details you'll have to get from Geoffrey Howard and Jennifer Carrington, but I've filled in as much as I can."

"And you're saying they killed Charles Carrington?" Lambert's tone defied him to agree.

"Yes. And they fitted up Lydden as what our American friends call a patsy beforehand. I inadvertently helped strengthen the case against him by seeing the connection between the safe combination and the Sherlock Holmes book."

Lambert sank into a chair like a half-set jelly. "You've got a gift for theories, my friend. Just go over this little lot for me. We've got all night if necessary."

"It won't take that long," Maltravers assured him. "It began when Howard met Gillian Carrington in Manchester. Probably he was her supplier. She must have told him about the Conan Doyle books and the safe combination. After she died, Howard decided to get those books.

"I don't know how long he'd known Jennifer, but he was certainly her boyfriend before she became a secretary at Carrington's firm. Obviously the first part of their plan was that she should marry him if possible, which turned out to be easier than they expected. She then started the affair with Lydden because he was stupid enough for what they wanted."

Lambert sat with the stillness of a soporific gorilla, but needle sharp eyes burned as he listened.

"The murder was very intricate," Maltravers went on. "Jennifer set off for Manchester all right, but returned shortly afterwards. She may have driven to Forton services on the M6 where Howard could have picked her up and brought her back in his car in case anyone spotted her red Fiesta. He'd spent the first part of the morning in the city buying things at busy shops and using her cash card at the bank to start building up her story that she'd been there all day.

"When Lydden arrived at Carwelton Hall at lunchtime she was there just as he said and they went to bed. That would have given Howard time to go to Lydden's house — Jennifer obviously lied about losing the key he gave her — and steal his shotgun. At the same time, he could have hidden the Conan Doyle books there."

"Just a minute," Lambert interrupted. "How do you know where the police found the books? We haven't revealed that."

"Jennifer Carrington told me. When she came to Brook Cottage after you released her, all sorts of things came out, almost certainly aimed at putting her in the clear and making things difficult for Lydden."

Lambert grunted, temporarily retreating as Maltravers continued.

"After Lydden left Carwelton Hall, Howard took Jennifer Carrington back to wherever her car was and she really went to Manchester. On her way to Timperley she called at Sherratt & Hughes and bought the book for Charles, using her credit card. She claimed that she went straight there after drawing the money from the bank in the morning, didn't she? I was in that shop today and it's so busy that the chances of the staff being able to remember if any one customer called in during the morning or afternoon can't be very great. It was a risk, but have you been able to confirm exactly what time she was actually there?"

Maltravers shrugged when Lambert did not reply. "Fair enough, it's not my place to ask you questions. However, Howard waited at Carwelton Hall for Carrington to return and killed him with Lydden's shotgun. I don't know exactly where the police found it later, but I'll bet it was somewhere highly suspicious where he might have hidden it himself. When Jennifer pointed you in Lydden's direction, he insisted he had met her at Carwelton Hall that lunchtime when she was apparently able to prove she had been in Manchester all day. Do you mind?"

Lambert's coconut head wobbled agreement as Maltravers produced his cigarettes; the superintendent declined one, but lit a pipe, the fallout from which manifested a serious breach of smoke pollution regulations.

"Then I came up with the point that Lydden could have guessed the safe combination from reading *The Attwater Firewitch*." Maltravers looked apologetic. "I'm afraid that misled you, but it seemed such a good idea at the time. They must have been counting on it as the final piece of evidence against him and it also deflected any suspicion from them. Charles himself told me Jennifer had never read the book and an old friend of hers who allegedly had never been to Carwelton Hall before the dinner party couldn't have, could he? If I hadn't worked out the significance of the murderer reading the book, they could have relied on the police realising it themselves eventually or found some other way of drawing it to their attention."

Maltravers tapped cigarette ash into a saucer on the table. "That's all I know, but you can find out the rest yourselves. What happened at Carwelton Hall tonight proves I'm right in any event."

Lambert stood up and asked Maltravers to wait. He returned after about ten minutes.

"According to Mr Howard's statement, you and Miss Davy went to Carwelton Hall this evening and accused Mrs Carrington of murder without any evidence," he said. "He was holding you at gunpoint prior to calling the police himself when Mrs Quinn's arrival caused a disturbance and you overpowered him."

"Balls." Maltravers gestured disparagingly. "That's desperation country. See what Jennifer's story is, they haven't had time to collude on this. And ask him about being a civil engineer in Nigeria for the past ten years, which was his story at the dinner party. My statement includes the name and address of a retired headmistress who has a flat in the same house in Manchester as he does and remembers meeting Jennifer Lloyd, as she then was, more than once within the last three years. Let him explain that lot away for starters."

"You've been very busy, Mr Maltravers." Lambert's pit-bottom voice had an accusing edge. "Why didn't you come to the police with all this at once instead of playing at amateur detectives?"

Maltravers looked regretful. "I've got no excuses for that. I wanted to prove I was right, but if I'd realised what Mrs Quinn was planning I'd have come to you immediately. Now I've had to give a statement as a witness to an assault as well as evidence of a murder. I'm sorry."

"Not just assault," Lambert corrected sternly. "Mrs Quinn may be charged with attempted murder and you could face charges as well. Withholding information from the police which could be of assistance in a murder enquiry is a very serious offence."

Maltravers looked at the impassive, unforgiving face of the law and sighed. "Can I ask for my presence at Carwelton Hall tonight to be taken into consideration? If I hadn't been there, Howard would probably have killed Charlotte Quinn when she attacked Jennifer and then they'd have made a run for it. I may have prevented a second murder."

"That's a matter for the Chief Constable," Lambert replied stonily and walked out. In his office he read the statements with growing resignation. There was a great deal the police would have to confirm, but Maltravers's story had a bizarre persuasiveness and the superintendent grudgingly accepted that it could actually be true.

"Bloody hell!" he groaned as he contemplated the prospect and consequences of being obliged to release Duggie Lydden.

A pale, moist dawn was forcing reluctant light into the sky by the time Maltravers and Tess left Kendal police station. The air was raw, the town was still and empty with a low mist smothering the River Kent as they drove through the silence across the grey stone bridge on their way back to Brook Cottage. They passed the hospital where Jennifer Carrington had recovered sufficiently for the police to begin questioning her; she was trying to blame Howard for the murder, claiming that he had said he only intended stealing the books. Iron-faced and numbed, Charlotte Quinn was being charged with grievous bodily harm as a holding operation. Lambert said the attempted murder charge could wait.

"Congratulations." Malcolm raised his glass as they sat round the fireplace in the lounge of Hodge Hill Hotel near Newby Bridge that evening. Maltravers had taken them all for dinner to the fifteenth-century manor house he regarded as the finest restaurant in Cumbria. "But for God's sake, you could both have ended up dead last night."

"Don't remind me," Maltravers admitted sourly. "I don't know if Tess will ever forgive me. And if I hadn't decided to go off and do my own thing, Charlotte might not have tried to kill Jennifer. Now I could end up helping send her to jail. I can't forgive myself for that."

Lucinda reached across from her chair and squeezed his hand. "Crime of passion perhaps? The courts might not be too hard on her. Stop blaming yourself, you weren't to know." He looked far from convinced.

"Lucinda's right," Tess added. "We survived and they might have got away with it if you hadn't worked it all out. I thought you'd gone mad when you started talking about dogs not barking in the night."

"But that was only the start," Maltravers remarked. "It was *The Attwater Firewitch* that helped me to think straight."

"How?" Malcolm asked.

"You've read it. Remember when Holmes is misled by what he thinks is a code and dashes off on a wild goose chase to Kirkby Lonsdale? After he realises his mistake, he says something to Watson about ignoring a simple truth because you've come up with some ingenious deduction which is so brilliant that you're dazzled by it.

"I did exactly the same thing. I was so self-satisfied about working out the numbers Carrington used for the safe and stitching up Lydden with it, that I didn't think it through. If he'd really stolen the books, he would have closed the safe behind him and nobody would have known about the theft until it was opened again. By then it would have been impossible to say when they had been taken and Lydden would not have been an automatic suspect. And he certainly wouldn't have waited for Charles to return home and shot him. What would have been the point?"

"When you put it like that, it's obvious," said Malcolm.

"As obvious as the fact that those numbers on the paper in *The Attwater Firewitch* were dates," Maltravers agreed. "But just like Holmes, I was looking in the wrong haystack."

"One thing I don't understand is why Howard was there for dinner that night," Tess remarked. "Surely Charles might have remembered him from Gillian's inquest."

"He didn't attend Gillian's inquest." Maltravers stretched forward to replace his dry sherry on the low table in front of them. "Malcolm and Lucinda told me that the night I arrived here. As far as Charles was concerned, he ceased to have a daughter from the moment he saw her dead. There was no risk of Howard being recognised, and I think he must have worked out that he had to go to Carwelton Hall and be seen there. He must have known that after the murder, police forensic experts would be digging up the drains in the library and those guys can tell your life story from the mud on your shoes. They'd have almost certainly found indications of the presence of everyone at that dinner party. If they'd come up with something specifically tied to Howard, it could have been explained by his having been among the guests.

"On top of that, there must be evidence all over the house of Howard being there from his previous visits to see Jennifer. Remember he was the one who asked Charles if he would show him round, which would have covered that as well."

"But if the police had got on to Howard, they'd have found everything we discovered," Tess objected.

"Of course they would, but with the case building up against Lydden they had little reason to suspect anyone else," Maltravers replied. "They haven't shown any interest in any of the rest of us who were there that night as far as I know."

"I haven't even been asked to give a statement," Malcolm put in.

"Precisely," Maltravers said. "On the other hand, if the police had chanced to find something which pointed to a man who should never have been at Carwelton Hall in the first place, they'd have become very suspicious. The chances weren't great, but they existed and Howard was intelligent enough to realise it. Crazy like a fox."

A waitress arrived to say their table was ready and they went through to the low, dark-panelled dining-room with its ancient black beams, oil-paintings and fire crackling in the immense open grate.

"What will happen to those books now?" Malcolm wondered as they began their meal.

"Well Jennifer certainly won't get her hands on them," Maltravers replied. "You can't benefit under your husband's will if you've been involved in killing him. Did Charles have any other family?"

"Not that we know of." Malcolm glanced at Lucinda for confirmation. "He had an older brother, but he was killed in the Normandy landings and wasn't married."

"Lot of deaths in that family," Maltravers observed, dipping his fork into his seafood cocktail. "Then he may have left everything to Jennifer, but she can't have it. Perhaps *The Attwater Firewitch* will finally be published. That would be an ironic sort of happy ending."

*

The ending — if any sequence of life involving love and death can be said to have such a thing — evolved over the next few weeks. Geoffrey Howard and Jennifer Carrington were jailed and, greatly to Maltravers's relief, Charlotte Quinn received a suspended prison sentence after her defence counsel made an impassioned plea to an understanding judge. For his part, Maltravers received a slap-on-the-wrist note from the Deputy Chief Constable of Cumbria, advising him that the police had decided not to take proceedings against him for failing to tell them what he had discovered immediately, but warning him that such actions constituted a very serious offence and any repetition of such behaviour would et cetera. The framed letter had joined his collection of bad reviews and rejection slips on the lavatory wall. Then Malcolm Stapleton wrote to him.

"It's a good news week on the *Chronicle*," he read. "Alan Morris — you remember our local vicar? — has been sent down for twelve months for ripping off the funds of several church charities. Apparently he'd been gambling on the horses for years and was up to his ears in debt to half the bookies in the north of England. Is nothing sacred? Several ladies of the parish are inconsolable.

"The other big story is Charles Carrington's will. He left everything to Jennifer, apart from some paintings for his old school and an edition of Cranmer's *Book of Common Prayer* which goes to Attwater church. The personal beneficiaries include Charlotte Quinn, who gets all the jewellery that belonged to his first wife. As we know, Jennifer can't inherit, but that should be covered by a standard clause under which everything was to be sold and the proceeds donated to a charity for drug addicts if she did not survive him by twenty-eight days.

"But the tragedy is *The Attwater Firewitch*. Charles left specific instructions that all ten volumes and the relevant letters were to be destroyed on his death (I quote from the will), 'to ensure that Sir Arthur Conan Doyle's wishes that the book should not be published will never be betrayed'. I've checked with Campbell, who was his executor, and he says it's been done; rather appropriately he burned them. At least we read it."

Maltravers smiled reflectively as he passed the letter across the breakfast table to Tess.

"Charles told me he'd made 'certain arrangements' about it," he said as she finished and looked at him sympathetically. "He didn't trust Jennifer. Anyway, there was an appalling mistake in it."

"Mistake? What?"

"For all practical purposes, eagles have no sense of smell. It would have been impossible to train one to hunt the way it happens in the book. But Conan Doyle moved Watson's wound from his arm to his leg — or perhaps it was the other way round, I can't exactly remember — in different stories and that didn't seem to matter either."

"And what about the photocopy?" Tess asked mildly. "Nobody knows you put it back in your pocket that night, do they? Apart from me."

Maltravers raised a surprised eyebrow. "You watch me too closely, madam. I didn't think anybody noticed."

"I had a feeling you weren't going to let it go. Your promise was that you would return it to Charles Carrington, not Jennifer."

"Exactly. I wanted to . . . I'm not sure. Not just to have it, although that's part of it of course, but to remind myself of a man who couldn't be bought. I don't meet many of them."

"What are you going to do with it?"

"Charles lent it to me because he trusted me. I'd certainly never try to publish it and the proof that it's the genuine article has been destroyed anyway." Maltravers shrugged. "It's just a literary curiosity now . . . perhaps I'll leave it to the grandchildren."

"Grandchildren?" Tess echoed innocently. "Don't children come first? And doesn't marriage. . . ?"

Abruptly aware of the implications of his remark, Maltravers imitated generations of (usually mendacious) newspaper reporters offered sexual favours while working on a vice ring exposé; he made an excuse and left. Tess's laughter followed him out of the room.